In *Confessions to a Stranger*, Danielle Grandinetti weaves a tale that is at once mysterious, suspenseful, romantic, and inspiring ... Filled with truths that made me ponder my own life, this novel is a lovely start to what is sure to be a wonderful series!

—Heidi Chiavaroli,
Carol Award-Winning Author of *The Orchard House*

Danielle Grandinetti has crafted a wonderful tale of suspense and romance that will keep you on the edge of your seat. With well-drawn characters authentic to the era, a gripping plot, and a strong message of hope, *Confessions to a Stranger* is a read I recommend!

—Misty M. Beller,
USA Today bestselling author of the Sisters of the Rockies

A Strike to the Heart is a compelling story. From the very first page, I was immersed into the thrilling action and remained gripped with intrigue until the satisfying ending. The romance escalated right along with the winding plot, creating a layered mystery that is sure to delight readers.

—Rachel Scott McDaniel,

Award-winning author of *The Mobster's Daughter*

Riveting from the first scene, *As Silent as the Night* offers a unique, edge-of-your-seat Christmas read ... A beautiful, gripping, and romantically suspenseful Christmas story you wouldn't be able to put down if you tried.

—Chautona Havig,
Author of *The Stars of New Cheltenham*

The Neighbor and the Gifts is a poignant tale that transforms a familiar carol into a stirring journey of faith, love, and danger ... For readers who love historical romance, mystery, and want a deeper meaning in their holiday stories—this one's for you.

—Natalie Walters,
bestselling and award-winning author of *Living Lies* and the *SNAP Agency* series

EYEWITNESS SKETCH

**Discover the Foundation
of Danielle's Bookish World**

Harbored in Crow's Nest
Confessions to a Stranger
Refuge for the Archaeologist
Escape with the Prodigal
Relying on the Enemy
Sheltered by the Doctor
Investigation of a Journalist

Bridge: His Boss's Little Sister

Unexpected Protectors
To Stand in the Breach
A Strike to the Heart
As Silent as the Night

For a complete list, visit
daniellegrandinetti.com/books

Eyewitness Sketch

Danielle Grandinetti

HEARTH SPOT PRESS

EYEWITNESS SKETCH

Copyright © 2026 by Danielle Grandinetti

Published by Hearth Spot Press

Kindle Book ISBN: 978-1-956098-51-8

E-Book ISBN: 978-1-956098-52-5

Paperback ISBN: 978-1-956098-53-2

All rights reserved.

No part of this publication may be reproduced, distributed, or transmitted in any form or by any means, including photocopying, recording, or other electronic or mechanical methods, without the prior written permission of the publisher, with the exception of limited quotations for use in reviews or promotional material or as permitted by U.S. copyright law. Neither may any unauthorized use of this publication be used to train generative artificial intelligence (AI) technologies. For permission requests, contact the author at daniellegrandinetti.com/contact

The story, all names, characters, and incidents portrayed in this production are fictitious. No identification with actual persons (living or deceased), places, buildings, and products is intended or should be inferred.

Scripture quotations are taken from the King James Version of the Bible

Book Cover by Roseanna White Designs

Author Picture: Abby Mae Tindal at Maeflower Photography

Editor: Sarah Hinkle

To my fellow creatives.

May you be "filled with wisdom of heart, to work all manner of work." (Ex. 35:35, KJV)

And he hath filled
him with the spirit
of God, in wisdom,
in understanding, and
in knowledge, and
in all manner of
workmanship.
Exodus 35:31, KJV

One

CHICAGO, ILL., SATURDAY, MARCH 7, 1931—They say curiosity killed the cat, which is why Gabriella Salatino preferred to let the cat keep her tongue. Silence was golden, as the saying went. However, she'd never managed to rein in her curiosity, which meant tonight might kill her.

Gabriella set her drawing pad and pencil on a chair near the closed garden doors in the farthest corner of the ballroom. The setting sun cast a golden sparkle over the snow-covered estate in Lincoln Park. One could almost believe that nothing existed beyond the hedgerows. Not Lake Michigan, not the dirty factories, not the growing homeless population.

She yearned to escape the stifling room and lifted

the strands of curly black hair that had escaped from where she'd pinned them at the back of her head. The unnatural electric light, the cloying variety of perfume, and the heat from the many bodies made the fabric of her straight, floor-length dress wrap itself around her ankles and dampness slip down her bare back. Perhaps she could crack open the door to the garden.

As an illustrative journalist for the Di Stasio Giornaliste Agency, she was on loan to *Illinois Life Magazine* to cover a series of spring charity events throughout the Chicago area. According to the managing editor, Katherine Arkley, Gabriella's sketches showed the elaborate lifestyle of the wealthy, allowing readers a voyeuristic look at their lives. Gabriella, however, preferred to look at her work as invisibly rooting out those using the less fortunate for personal gain while shedding light on the growing need throughout the city, all behind the safety of her pencil. It's why she joined Ali Di Stasio's agency, though being a fellow Italian-American was how she discovered the woman in the first place.

Gabriella searched the room for another tableau to capture on her blank page. Susan Brink, hostess and founder of the Brink Scholarship Fund, held court on the far side of the room. Her silver hair twisted up, revealing a long neck on which hung a necklace of diamonds—the

Brink Diamond Necklace. Susan only donned it when she asked her guests to open their wallets.

"See anything notable?" Billy Holland, the lead society columnist at *Illinois Life* leaned close to Gabriella's ear, his breath causing an unwelcome shiver. He ran a finger down her bare arm. "Go to dinner with me again."

She froze. This was why she kept words locked away. Men took one look at her exotic skin and thought her a loose woman. Worse? They got angry when she said no. She forced herself to relax. This was Billy Holland. He was one of the few people who knew Ali as both the head of a journalism agency and the wife of one of the Astor Street elite. He was safe, and a friend, which was why she'd agreed to his suggestion last week.

"It was a moment of weakness, Mr. Holland." Saturday had been the seventh anniversary of her mother's death. Vulnerable, she hadn't had the courage to decline Billy's simple dinner invitation. She hadn't meant to encourage something more than one nice supper. She never did. But people flustered her, especially when her insides were in turmoil. Next time, she'd be stronger. Or just say nothing at all.

"I know. You and your colleagues are women above measure." He slumped into the chair beside her, his black suit crumpling.

Gabriella frowned. "You deserve a woman above measure, Billy."

He waved her admonition away. "How about you toss me a story? Arkley has been complaining my stories aren't juicy enough."

She lifted her pad and pencil and sat in their place. She could talk about work. Maybe. Sometimes, words tangled in her throat and refused to leave. "I haven't seen one yet." She tapped her pencil on her drawing pad and scanned the crowd.

"Wait." Gabriella sat up, peering through dancing couples. "Who's that with George Zander? By the punch table."

"George Zander is here?" Billy jumped to his feet, nearly bumping her off her chair. "Who is he with?"

"Why don't you be a journalist and find out," she muttered, then pinned her lips closed, hoping Billy hadn't heard her. If only she had a silver tongue to match her curiosity. She wanted the answer to her question, too.

As Billy sauntered away, Gabriella focused on the couple, her pencil recreating their likeness on her blank page. Middle-aged but unmarried and still good-looking, George Zander flashed a confident smile. No one, including the local journalists, knew how he had made his millions. He claimed it was due to investing in the stock market. Yet after last year's crash? She had doubts since his living standard hadn't seemed to change.

The woman he spoke to appeared to be half his age. She wore a formal black silk dress with a plunging back. When she turned and smiled, Gabriella mentally captured her picture to recreate as a sketch—a sketch of the notorious Molly Zander, George's only child. Molly usually frequented speakeasies and clubs, followed mercilessly by a band of men begging for her attention, not charity dinners for education.

Movement in the background caused Gabriella to flip to a new page. People kept moving through her line of sight, blocking her view with blurry forms of shimmery purple, dazzling blue, or silky black. Gabriella shifted to her right to get a better angle. Charles Brink? What was Susan's husband doing hiding in the shadows outside the open garden door behind Mr. Zander? Her pencil copied the image onto the page.

Another man greeted him. A black suit like all the other men. Perfectly trimmed black hair. Not Billy Holland, then. *Please turn around. Turn ... yes!* She sucked in a breath. Thomas Cook? Gabriella sketched him into her scene, then turned the page to hide the image, her mind reeling as she pieced together this information.

Thomas Cook was one of the most eligible bachelors in

Chicago. Dark-eyed, well-built, and as smooth as cream. Wealthy, too. But he wasn't known for his charity. He was a ruthless businessman determined to become one of the richest in the nation. Why come to a charity event? Why meet with Charles Brink? He was up to something, and Gabriella doubted it came from the goodness of his heart.

"You look perplexed, darling." The smooth male voice sent a shudder down her spine.

"Good evening, Mr. Cook." How long had she been woolgathering? Did he know she'd seen him? She pressed her clammy palms to her sketch pad, praying he wouldn't snatch it and see what she'd drawn.

"Are you enjoying the gala, Miss Salatino?" His hand pressed Gabriella's shoulder.

"Yes, sir." She adjusted her long skirt, the action shifting her away from him.

"You seemed rather lost." His smile dazzled. Most girls would swoon if Thomas Cook looked at them like he did at her. She closed her fist around her pencil. His smile hid a shark.

"What are you doing at Mrs. Brink's fundraiser?" The words jumped out, and her embarrassment heated her through. Curiosity would be the death of her!

His eyes twinkled with a flirtatious glimmer. "All the local businessmen were invited; why wouldn't I be here?"

Gabriella wrinkled her nose. "You don't attend charity events." Oh, had she said that out loud, too? He could make assumptions she didn't intend.

"Perhaps I heard you would be here." He leaned forward, and she leaned away until the chair back stopped her parry.

"I cover all the charity galas, Mr. Cook. It's my job."

He took Gabriella's hand, the one not clutching her pencil like a dagger. "What's a dame like you gotta work for? Let's grab a drink. I know this cozy joint—"

"No!" Gabriella snatched her hand away. Why did he keep asking her? Never mind that buying alcohol was illegal.

"I won't stop until you're married." He leaned over her. "Maybe, maybe when you lasso a steady man."

Aha! Finally, a way out. "Well, I do. Have a beau, that is."

Gabriella wasn't being courted, but she would happily fabricate a boyfriend if it meant getting Thomas Cook to leave her alone. Ever since they were introduced last year at another gala, he'd been determined for her to agree to a date.

Mr. Cook rolled his eyes. "Then why isn't he here with you?"

Gabriella's mind churned. Thomas Cook hadn't

met a problem he couldn't resolve or an obstacle he couldn't overcome, and for some reason, he had turned that willpower on Gabriella. For the briefest moment, Gabriella considered caving simply to get information—he was definitely up to something, and she wanted to know what it was. But she also knew he'd want more if she gave him even a sliver.

Lord, please give me courage. "My man hates these types of events."

"I want to talk with him and prove he exists." Mr. Cook grabbed her elbow, pulling her up, and she flinched, but he tugged her along in such a way that it would create a scene to disengage. "We'll use Brink's telephone."

She clutched her sketch pad like a shield as he led her into Mr. Brink's quiet office. She'd opened the door to this mess. Perhaps this could end the obsession Mr. Cook had with her. But who would agree to be the other half of her fake relationship? She could have used Billy Holland, but the poor man would get the wrong idea. She could call her best friend's husband, but he sounded too much like the mayor and father of three that he was. And Mr. Cook would recognize his voice, seeing that they were both wealthy Chicago businessmen.

However, her best friend's brother? She sighed. Andri would do.

She lifted the candlestick telephone's receiver and asked to be connected. Mr. Brink could cover the long-distance charge.

"Andri Jóhannsson?" Mr. Cook sounded condescendingly irritated when the operator asked whom she should ring up. "Never heard of him."

Two rings, three. Finally, Andri answered. "What, Gabriella?" He was the only man who thought her pesky, and while he wanted nothing to do with her, he'd protect her like a little sister. Of course, he was the only man who invaded her dreams.

"Just wanted to call my boyfriend." Gabriella fabricated a perky tone he'd know was false, emphasizing *boyfriend*. If only she could crawl under the carpet and hide. How did she get herself into these scrapes? "I'm working the charity event tonight, you know."

Please say something so I know you're not upset with me.

"Give that to me." Mr. Cook snagged the receiver out of her hands. "Who is this?"

Gabriella covered her burning face with her hands, her mortification complete. Andri already thought of her as a younger sister, a girl, not a woman. But he was the only one she trusted not to get the wrong idea.

"Who I am is none of your concern." Andri's bass voice crackled through the earpiece loud enough for Gabriella to hear the deadly edge to his words.

"Not until you confirm how long Gabriella's been your girl," Mr. Cook demanded.

Gabriella pressed into the wall, tears stinging her eyes. She'd wanted to be Andri's girl for as long as she could remember. Once upon a time she had never felt shy or ill-at-ease around him. That changed seven years ago, and tonight would only make it worse. Why had she thought this was a good idea?

"I don't believe you're her boyfriend." Mr. Cook grinned at her like a cat toying with a bird. Or was it the mouse who got the cheese?

Andri's voice rumbled through the phone, but Gabriella heard no distinct words. Then Mr. Cook's smile faded, and, without a word, he tossed Gabriella the earpiece like a hot coal. With words unfit for a gentleman scorching the air, he stormed off.

"What did you say to him?" Gabriella whispered into the phone. "He hightailed it out of here like he was about to lose half his millions."

"That just confirms he's no good." Andri's exasperated sigh was one she'd heard directed at her all her life. "Now, what's going on, Gabby? Do I need to come down there? Do you need me to come get you?"

She wanted to say yes, but he only asked because he saw

her as a helpless little sister. Anyway, he was three hundred miles away. "I'll be fine. You can stand down. I don't need a policeman."

"Gabriella—"

"I'm fine, Andri." She swallowed back the emotion clogging her voice. "Thank you."

She bid him goodbye and hung up the receiver. If only she could hang up her childhood feelings toward him as easily.

Two

Heima Island deputy police officer Andri Jóhannsson jammed the earpiece back on the hook of his wall box telephone. Gabriella Salatino would be the death of him. She was the only girl who could wiggle under his skin like a burr. She was also the only woman he genuinely enjoyed being around. But she was his sister's best friend, so his job was to protect her, even from himself.

He finished buttoning his coat before pulling a dark knit cap well over his ears to cover his light hair and whistling for his German Shepherd, Freya, to follow. Together, they jogged toward the stretch of shore on the opposite side of the island from the Heima Island Lighthouse, which faced Plum Island directly across Death's Door.

Technically, Heima Island was on the Green Bay side of the Door Peninsula, not in Lake Michigan. Nestled to the northwest of the peninsula and the southwest of Washington Island, Heima Island was a welcome sight to mariners headed for Green Bay, Wisconsin, a sign they were safely on their way home.

The passage between the mainland and Washington Island was one of the most dangerous straits in the United States. Since the Sturgeon Bay Ship Canal at the base of the peninsula had been built before the turn of the century, the islands hadn't seen as many ships go down while threading the Porte des Morts. Even though it affected Heima Island's economy as the last safe spot before entering the Great Lakes, it was a blessing.

Tonight, spring remained a dream as the temperatures hovered near zero, thanks to a brisk wind blowing in from Lake Superior, and spending hours on the back section of the island meant that if he didn't bundle up, he'd turn into an ice block before the suspected criminals appeared.

"Do you think they'll show?" Andri asked his boss and only colleague as he settled beside the giant man in the dark brush along the shoreline.

"That's the gossip." Chief Gunnar Michelsen looked more like a gray-haired bear than an old-time law enforcement officer. Not that Andri looked much different. They were both large men who intimidated strangers. Locals, not so much. Michelsen had a doughy center, and Andri would forever be the reverend's troublemaking son.

Andri flexed his cold fingers inside his woolen mittens, the thought of troublemaking bringing his mind back to Gabby's odd telephone call and snatching his concentration. What had she gotten herself into now? She was smart, with a memory to rival granite, and the ability to draw unlike anyone he'd ever met. But the girl had no common sense, and he wasn't the only boy—or man, now—who was captured by her beauty.

So, who was the man harassing her this time? If he didn't need to sit here, enforcing the Volstead Act, he'd show up at her gala, which would embarrass her into never speaking with him again. He'd risk it if it kept her safe, but the loss would hurt more than he cared to admit.

"If we can raid this shipment and get to the seller, we can stop the influx of alcohol," the chief was saying. How long had he been talking while Andri's mind was on Gabby? "And that will make the town happy."

"These bootleggers must not know anything about the area. Anywhere else in Wisconsin, they'd receive no opposition." Frankly, Andri didn't think the Noble Experiment was working. It sure hadn't saved Gabby's mother.

Next to him, Freya whimpered. Andri touched the two-year-old German Shepherd's head to quiet her. She wasn't an official police dog, like he'd heard were being used in places like New York, but the chief let her come along on raids like this. Andri had been a Heima Island policeman for over five years already, and Freya felt like a partner now, especially since their police force consisted of only him and the chief.

Her whimper turned into a low rumble. Andri pushed distraction aside and focused on the water. A light was bobbing on the bay, heading for shore. He tapped his finger on his lips, his signal to quiet her. Rustling came from the left. Freya's muscles tightened against Andri's leg. Despite the cold, sweat ran down Andri's temple.

Two armed figures jogged to the water's edge, meeting the shallow boat. They set the lantern on shore while they helped lift four barrels onto the bank. Again, why unload here where a town of full-blown teetotalers wouldn't allow a drop of the stuff to pass their borders? Andri lifted his binoculars.

"Armed," Michelsen grunted beside him.

"Two Tommy guns." This wasn't Chicago. It didn't make sense that men such as these were here on Heima Island.

"Let me see." Michelsen yanked away the binoculars.

"We're not prepared for this." Andri tightened a grip on Freya's lead. She wouldn't attack unless he gave the command, but he needed the added security for his peace of mind.

"We'll follow before we arrest them." The chief shoved the binoculars back at Andri. "I want this whole operation shut down."

Born and raised as a pastor's son on Heima Island, Andri knew his father, like the majority of people on Heima Island, refused to allow the Eighteenth Amendment to be broken within the town limits. But neither was Heima Island, with its four hundred residents, the cesspool of crime residents feared it could become. Yet something in the chief's tone set him on edge.

"Sir," Andri spoke as softly as possible. "Do you know more about this than I do?"

"If you'd been listening instead of dreaming about you-know-who, you might know a bit more than you do at the moment." Michelsen glared at the men who lifted a barrel to each shoulder.

Embarrassment washed through him as he eyed the Tommy guns hanging down their chests. His mind replayed Gabby's call and the threat he'd delivered to the man giving her unwanted attention. Why else would

Gabby feign being his girl? Once upon a time, he thought his childhood crush could become a future. Except he'd messed up. Now, a faceless threat was all the rescue she would trust him to make.

"They've rounded the bend." The chief interrupted Andri's prayer for Gabby. "Take Freya, but keep your distance. We want the buyers, not the go-between."

Andri gave a nod, then gave Freya the command and followed as low as possible.

Freya tracked the smugglers back towards the center of town. The closer they got, the more confused Andri became. The Main Street shop owners had collectively shut down a speakeasy last year and run the owner out of town. Andri wished he could ask the chief to repeat himself, but the large man couldn't keep up with Freya's lanky speed.

As it was, the cold air made it a challenge for Andri to keep up with her. Straight down Main Street, she led him. The brazenness of the smugglers confounded him. Had the town's focus on prosecuting the Volstead Act blinded them to the signs of bootlegging happening in their midst?

The religious history of Heima Island was a large part of the overwhelming support for the Volstead Act. His father had led the charge and continued to encourage the residents to uphold the law. But Andri had heard rumors of a growing contingent of shoreline residents who wanted to join the rest of the state in working toward changing the amendment. While Heima Island didn't have a brewery, as other cities in Wisconsin did, these outliers wanted a pharmacy willing to dispense alcohol, a brewery providing a brewing kit, or simply a speakeasy. Andri had no opinion on the laws—his job was to enforce, not debate. He simply despised the stuff because it had taken Gabby's mother from her.

Freya's low growl signaled a warning. Andri dropped to a knee and drew his pistol. A shadow darted away, leaving a darker spot in the middle of Main Street. Andri approached carefully. It was a barrel. A single barrel. One that looked eerily similar to one taken from the boat that had moored on their shores. The strong, sharp smell of pure moonshine wafted up to greet him.

Freya sniffed around the bottom, then looked up at Andri.

"Aye, you did good, girl." Andri scratched behind her ear. It wasn't Freya's fault she followed the scent of this barrel since the smugglers apparently divided their take. He should have guessed their plan since the trail had led to such a conspicuous place.

He rested his hands on his belt. Despite everything,

bootlegging had come to Heima Island.

Three

As soon as Gabriella returned to the Di Stasio building, she changed from her gown to a warm, flannel nightdress. While Ali owned the building, she had never lived there. Instead, the downstairs served as the agency offices, and the upstairs could house up to six female journalists. Ali only employed female journalists.

Gabriella let down her curls and slipped her sore feet into homemade slippers from Mrs. Jóhannsson. At the moment, only four journalists made their home here but none of the others were in residence. Caroline Wagoneer, an undercover investigative journalist, was out following some sort of corruption scandal. Emma Hancock, a sports journalist, had just left for Houston to watch a baseball exhibition game involving the Chicago White Sox and a

New York team. And Lena Carney, a political journalist, had yet to return from Washington, D.C., where she traveled to witness Congress officially designate *The Star Spangled Banner* as the national anthem and President Hoover sign it into law.

Ali had offered to send someone over so Gabby didn't have to stay alone, but Lena was expected back tomorrow and Gabriella was glad to be by herself. She turned up her lantern and snuggled under her quilt to draw.

If she didn't finish her sketches before she slept, the images would grow fuzzy around the edges, almost as if they took on the crackle of a moving picture. Despite needing to work more before she slept, this was her favorite part of the job. Her mind would wander over the evening as she recreated it with only her pencil. She would always remember something she could pass on to writers like Billy Holland or her female colleagues.

On the first page, a fresh image of Mrs. Brink quickly rose with soft eyes and a steel spine.

On the second page, her husband joined her with the strong air of a successful businessman. Sixty-four years old, married thirty-nine years, he was a partner in a manufacturing firm in the city. But he hadn't gotten his money from his job. He'd married it. Mrs. Brink came from old money and had inherited everything when her father died forty years ago. She had dedicated her life to creating her charity and gave several scholarships a year to female students.

Then, George Zander and his daughter. Other guests she'd watched dance the night away. Until the face of Thomas Cook formed beneath her pencil.

Usually, she sketched him alongside one of the various girls he brought to these galas. Reason number five-eighty-two why she would never agree to dinner with him. All she'd read about him were articles about his latest girl, clothing, and ruthless business practices. Though what business he was in, no one said.

Tonight, however, the picture she created was of only his face. A tremor ran through her as she appraised her work.

When she sketched from memory like this, her illustrations were less a photograph of a moment and more a meshing of impressions she morphed into a single image. She relied heavily on that internal intuition, and editors always preferred her after-event illustrations more than the ones she created during the event itself.

This was one sketch she would burn before anyone else saw it. The expression in Mr. Cook's eyes was one of cold calculation. The kind that would do anything, even take a life, to get what he wanted. She'd seen that look in one other person's eyes—the man who murdered her mother.

She shuddered again as she tore out the page and clambered out of bed. Chief Michelsen was the only one who knew she'd witnessed her mother's murder. Not even Ali knew. Everyone else thought she'd come upon the scene after the killer had fled, and she let the assumption hold. The man hadn't seen her, and she hadn't recognized him. But she'd given the chief a sketch, and she'd tell him if she ever saw his face again. She never had.

For now, her questions had her donning her robe and quietly descending the stairs to the community telephone in the downstairs hall. The operator put her through and Billy answered on the second ring.

"Change your mind about tonight, doll?"

Unlike Mr. Cook, Billy's flirtations were as harmless as a friendly retriever. "I rang to find out what you learned about Molly Zander."

Billy sighed. "Nothing. She stuck close to her father and was remarkably well-behaved. Think she's turning over a new leaf?"

Do apple trees suddenly grow pears? Gabriella traced a flower on the wallpaper. "There's something there."

"Arkley won't let you investigate, Salatino. She only wants us covering society pieces." Another sigh. "And do you really think your boss will sanction looking into this? I know it's a secret, so fill in the gaps: letting one of her girls investigate a rival isn't wise."

He meant one of her husband's rivals, and Billy was probably right. Except ... "I'm curious." Gabriella tried to keep her voice light as she stared at the sketch she'd created of Thomas Cook. She'd toss it in the fire before returning upstairs.

"You sure you're not seeing shadows where there aren't any?" Billy might flirt, but he cared. Another reason she hadn't said no to him taking her out on a date last week. "You're not an investigative reporter."

"Just because I don't use a typewriter—" Like Caroline, and Emma, and Lena. She pinned her lips closed.

"You use your sketchpad to watch the elite at fancy dinners. Not report on a prohibition raid."

Pain shot through her heart. Her mother died because she'd stumbled on a bootlegging ring. "Billy ..."

"Fine." The man huffed. "I'll admit something seemed off between Zander and Brink. They went out of their way to avoid each other."

Sunlight broke through the clouds. "You're already investigating this, aren't you?"

Billy chuckled. "You've got good instincts behind that sketch pad of yours."

Gabriella smiled. "Not a date, but can we compare notes over brunch?"

"Ten at that cafe by the theatre?" Which was across from where she attended church services at eleven.

"Thank you, Billy. I'll be there."

Four

Andri woke to darkness outside his bedroom window. He blinked. Exhaustion was heavy after being up most of the night. Why was he awake?

Ring.

Ah. Telephone.

Andri scrambled out of bed, disrupting Freya, who lay on a rug beside it, and ran down the hall to the telephone box. "Jóhannsson."

"Why did Tabby just get home?" Mother.

"Hello to you, too." Andri rubbed his forehead. What time was it anyway?

"Stop your nonsense." She lowered her voice, not that she could hide what she said on the party line. "She won't tell me, and something is different this time."

Visions of the moonshine barrels smuggled onto the beach last night filled his head. "Different, how?"

"Just speak with her, please. I don't believe she'll be joining us at services today."

Andri agreed and replaced the ear cone with a long sigh. At one time, he'd been the prodigal son. The reverend's child everyone sighed over. His middle sister, Ruth, was an angel and everyone assumed Tabitha, the baby of the family, would be more like her older sister than her older brother. But the last few months had been proving everyone wrong. She stayed out late, flirted with boys, and often skipped Sunday service.

His mantle clock struck the hour. Six in the morning. No point going back to bed since dawn would arrive shortly. Freya followed him into the kitchen, where he stoked the stove fire. Was his sister involved with whatever smuggling they saw last night? Could she have been one of the people they followed? No. She was a strain on their parents, but she couldn't be into something so dangerous as bootlegging.

He filled the kettle with the icy water from his kitchen pump and set it on the stove, then stuffed his feet in his boots, donned his heavy winter coat, and joined Freya outside for their morning ablutions. He usually didn't mind having an outdoor privy. He'd experienced an indoor one a few times, and they were all the same in the end. But he dreamed of adding indoor plumbing to his little house on frosty mornings like this.

He'd purchased the land and built his cabin five years ago when he moved back to Heima Island after time on the mainland peninsula corrected his downward path. This was his sanctuary now, his place of retreat. The only thing it lacked was the touch of a woman.

Thoughts of Gabby swirled around him like the icy wind as he returned to the house. Had she gotten home safely after the gala last night? Would there be a way to ask Ruthie at services today?

Freya's bark brought Andri back to the moment. He'd barely fed his partner when his telephone rang for the second time that morning. This time, it was Michelsen.

Lydia Abraham's restaurant had been robbed.

Fifteen minutes later, Andri's breath puffed out in a white cloud as he stood beside Chief Michelsen outside Lydia's Kitchen, Freya at his feet. Red checkered curtains covered the lower half of the windows, blocking his view inside. "What evidence is there?"

"Till was open and the cash gone." Michelsen rubbed gloved hands together. "Why do criminals have to operate on the coldest day of the spring?"

"It's technically still winter." Andri rested his hands on

his belt.

Freya shifted to her haunches, leaning against Andri's leg. It was too cold to stand out here, but they needed a conversation away from gossiping ears.

Andri crossed his arms. "Was there evidence of a break-in?"

Michelsen glanced around, as did Andri. The sun had just begun to rise above the Lake Michigan horizon, and dawn provided enough light to see they were alone.

"I want Freya to give a sniff around," Michelsen said.

Freya raised her nose at the sound of her name.

"You think she'll find the bootlegged alcohol?"

"Alcohol!" Miss Lydia Abraham screeched from her restaurant's doorway.

Andri and Michelson winced. Freya barked.

"Get that dog away from me." Miss Lydia pulled her hands to her chin. Frail and gaunt, prematurely gray, with glasses sitting low on her nose, she looked to be in her seventies. But Andri knew she was younger than his parents, who hadn't yet reached sixty.

"We want to cover all possibilities, Lydia." Chief Michelsen put on his best public relations voice. "We'll catch whoever did this."

She sniffed.

"Is there anyone who would want to make trouble for

you?" Andri rested his palm on Freya's head.

"Trouble?"

Andri tried not to cringe. Her voice always grated on him, but today it sounded like nails on a chalkboard. Even Freya let a whine escape. Andri scratched behind her ear.

Michelsen approached Miss Lydia and gently cupped her elbow. "I'm sure no one would want to purposefully cause you any undue stress." Andri could take lessons in compassion from his boss.

But Miss Lydia snorted. "Mr. Jakobsen would love to see me out of business. Hates female business owners, you know."

"Really?" Joel Jakobsen plowed into the group, hair disheveled, vest buttons miss-aligned, and coat flapping open. "I just want you to let me run my business my way. I wouldn't damage *yours*."

Freya looked Jakobsen over, then adjusted to her haunches. Interesting. Andri trusted her instincts, and she felt no animosity from Joel. They'd gone through school in the same grade, but Joel was always the teacher's pet. Intelligent, well-behaved, and ambitious. Andri was none of those.

"You hate my kitchen." Miss Lydia stabbed a bony finger at Jakobsen.

"I don't like the décor." Joel scrunched his nose as if the

word 'décor' smelled like rotten fruit.

"You want to sell … alcohol." Miss Lydia covered her mouth and widened her eyes as if the very word were a bad one.

"I'm a chef, not the community's conscience." Joel glared at her. "It's not my place to dictate what other people eat or drink."

Miss Lydia stepped back as if Joel had slapped her. "You see, Chief, he wants to ruin my business."

Andri barely resisted rolling his eyes. These two had been feuding since Joel took over his family's restaurant. They'd been the only eateries on the island for as long as Andri could remember, so he couldn't understand Miss Lydia's annoyance.

Regardless, it was too cold to stand out here arguing. He turned to his boss. "Chief, can Freya go in yet?"

"You think she has alcohol stashed in that place?" Joel laughed. "She won't even use it to cook!"

"How could you suggest such a thing?" Miss Lydia glared at Joel like the upstart she thought he was.

"Citizens, please." Chief Michelsen held up his hands. "Let my officer do his job."

Andri took that as his cue to escape, and Freya trotted after him, quickly passing him in her eagerness.

Andri followed her into Lydia's Kitchen. He released her

lead, gave her a command, and she lifted her nose in the air. He stayed close. They wove around the dozen or so tables covered in red checkered cloth. The mural on the wall gave the impression that the room was a breakfast nook in a home best featured in *Good Housekeeping*. Through the swinging doors and into the kitchen they went. Worktable, wood stove, sink pump, electric refrigerator.

Andri drifted behind Freya as she passed by the cupboard. So far, Lydia Abraham was as clean as she claimed. Andri knew the chief was covering his bases, especially after the bootlegging shipment last night, but he seriously doubted Miss Lydia was involved.

At least, he doubted it until Freya's tail went stiff. She pawed at the back door. Andri pushed it open for her, and she trotted down the back steps to the root cellar door. When she scratched at the doors, Andri rested his hand on his pistol, hollering for the chief to join him. Miss Lydia followed Michelson to the rear of the building, and Joel joined them despite Lydia's protests.

"Do we have your permission to search the cellar?" Chief Michelsen asked Miss Lydia.

"Because the dog wants to go down there?" She scowled. "How's that going to find who stole my money?"

"You afraid they're going to find something they shouldn't?" Joel poked at his competition. Andri gave him a look.

"It is entirely up to you, Lydia," Michelsen said. "You asked us to investigate. Our investigation has led here."

"No." She shook her head. "Too many prying eyes. I have a business to run, and this is preventing me from opening as usual."

"Are you sure?" Chief Michelsen pressed.

"Absolutely." Lydia gave a decisive nod.

Andri tried to catch the chief's eye, but Michelsen gave a subtle shake of his head. Freya looked up at him when Andri placed a hand on her head. She'd done good. And Andri knew he'd done right by calling the chief rather than opening the cellar without permission. But something felt ... off about the whole situation.

However, in a matter of a few minutes, Lydia had effectively kicked everyone out of her restaurant. Joel Jakobsen shrugged with feigned indifference as he returned to his business. Michelsen ordered Andri to report to the office after services, and Andri led Freya home despite the troubled feeling churning in his gut.

He had too many questions and not enough answers.

FIVE

Gabriella stood just inside the cafe door, her clutch under her arm, her ever-present satchel of sketch supplies over her shoulder. She looked around for the third time, then checked her pocket watch. Where was Billy? They'd agreed on ten, and it was now twenty past, and the waitress kept giving her sidelong looks of sympathy.

Perhaps Billy had overslept. It would be the height of impropriety for her to visit an unmarried male colleague at his home, but her curiosity combined with her worry overcame that good sense. She would check on him. After all, she knew he lived in a boarding house not far away, and the matron should still be there since she attended the same protestant church as Gabriella—even though other Italians in the neighborhood attended St. Mark's Church across from the Di Stasio building. With only one church on her home of Heima Island, going to a Protestant church was all Gabby had ever known.

The five-minute walk had Gabriella chilled to the bone. Worse, when she got to the door, no one answered. Too cold not to try, she twisted the doorknob and found it unlocked. *Thank you.* The whispered prayer slipped out as she entered the homey hall. Silence greeted her. The type of silence that set her nerves on edge.

Right about now, Andri would be demanding she telephone him, or at least a local police precinct. But there was nothing specific to report, and Andri was too far away to help. Ruthie would wink, link their arms, and encourage Gabriella's curiosity. Everyone thought the middle Jóhannsson child was an innocent and Gabriella the instigator, but the girls knew the truth.

"Billy?" she called, too softly at first. Then louder. No answer. Dare she find his rooms? The thought heated her cheeks, giving her courage to raise her voice. "Billy Holland, where are you? Why aren't you answering your door?"

A creak. A crash. And then the unmistakable sound of a gun firing.

Gabriella clapped her hands over her mouth to hold in a

scream and a masked man appeared at the top of the stairs, a gun in his hand. In an instant, she ran down the hall, through the empty kitchen—where was everyone?—then out the back door. Where now?

Heavy footsteps followed. She ran down the back alley and turned the first corner as a gunshot echoed behind her. Chipped brick pieces bit into her neck and she heard the man following still.

She ran faster, her satchel slapping her hip. She dodged into a narrow opening, then around another corner. When she spotted a tiny hidey-hole halfway down the passage, she slipped inside.

Gabriella curled into a ball, knees tucked up to her chin. She shivered. No, trembled. From cold. From fear. Then, she heard the man's steps slow as he came upon the entrance to the narrow passage. Would he turn?

Please, please, go on your way.

A moment later, his steps retreated. She counted to fifty, then another fifty, until her breathing calmed and the cold became unmanageable. Then she crept from the passage. With no sign of the intruder, she hurried back to the boardinghouse. She'd use the telephone in the hall to call Ali, then the police, but she had to check on Billy. If there was a chance he still lived, she couldn't waste any time.

She re-entered the kitchen, then quietly closed the door

and locked it for good measure. Before she went further, she tuned her ears to any sound. If the gun-toting man had returned, she'd hear him, wouldn't she? Instead, banging came from the root cellar beneath her feet. She knelt and eased open the door in the plank floor to find the matron Mrs. Green and a woman in a maid uniform hog-tied on the cellar floor.

"Are you alright?"

Mrs. Green managed to say Billy's name around the gag in her mouth. The fear and concern in her eyes had Gabriella agreeing to find him before releasing them. But if the man returned ... Gabriella shuddered ... She couldn't leave them without a means to defend themselves.

A quick glance round the kitchen and her gaze landed on a knife. She left it with Mrs. Green and the maid, then hurried up the stairs. But when she reached the landing, her feet slowed. "Billy?"

Silence. *You can do this. He's not your mother. He might not be dead.* But then a smell reached her that turned her insides. Using a single finger, she pushed open the first door in the hall and gagged. Billy Holland lay in a pool of blood, a hole in his chest. She was too late. He'd been dead before he fell. Just like her mama.

Gabriella pulled up her skirt as she leaned over Billy's body. There was no doubt he was dead, but she had to check. He deserved that much. She bit her lip as she attempted to keep her stomach contents in place. No pulse.

A tear, no, two or three, slipped down her cheeks. She backed out of the room and met Mrs. Green in the hall as the matron was lifting the candlestick telephone from the entry table. Gabriella pinned her lips shut to keep from asking to call Ali first. It would be highly irregular, but both Ali and Carrie had instilled in her a strong distrust of the police.

Instead she leaned against the wall, closed her eyes. What did that man want with Billy? Who would want Billy dead? And why, oh why, did *she* have to be the one who found him?

"Yes," the matron was saying. "I would like to report a break-in and ... Gabriella is he ... ?"

Gabriella nodded and Mrs. Green handed her the ear cone. No choice but to take it, her fingers trembled as she held it to her ear. "Y-yes?"

"You are the eyewitness?" asked the gravelly voice on the line.

"Yes, sir." If she approached this conversation as a professional, it would help. "My name is Gabriella Salatino, a journalist with the Di Stastio Giornalist Agency and a colleague of ..."

Her surroundings faded as her memory replayed the scene of Billy's murder against the back of her eyelids. Usually, that skill served her well, but right now, she hated it. Beyond Billy's lifeless body, his room had been a disaster. Pillows ripped open. Books tossed on the floor, even a potted plant had been upended, dirt covering the carpet. What had the man been looking for?

Cold hands took something from Gabriella's fingers, and she realized she'd forgotten the officer on the line. Mrs. Green spoke, whether to Gabriella or the officer, Gabriella didn't know. The words did not reach her mind as it continued the moving picture. Billy's cluttered desk had papers strewn, but something wasn't right. Perhaps she would have found her way back to look at what her mental picture missed, but gentle hands directed her to the kitchen.

By the time the maid settled a warm teacup in Gabriella's hands, she'd become aware enough to hear Mrs. Green greet someone at the front door. Fear shot through her before she recognized the gravelly voice of the officer from the telephone. Still, unease inched up her spine. She needed to ask Ali if this policeman could be trusted.

She left the cup on the kitchen table and eased down the hall, running the tips of her fingers over the wallpaper to keep herself mentally in the present.

"Are you Miss Salatino?" the gravelly-voiced officer turned from Mrs. Green to eye her approach. He wore a tan trench coat and black bowler. Had black hair and a kind smile.

Gabriella nodded, her fingers twisting together so that she wished she hadn't left the teacup in the kitchen.

"I'm Detective Arthur." The man approached Gabriella as she would an injured animal. Slowly, gently. "This is Officer Wilson. He will wait with you while I have a look around. Then I will have questions for you, alright?"

Gabriella didn't know what to answer. She wanted Ali. Or Andri. If this had happened on Heima Island, he'd be the officer responding. With Chief Michelsen. She could trust them.

The matron wrapped an arm around Gabriella's waist and settled her on the parlor couch before leaving her alone. Officer Wilson stood at the door with his hands on his belt, feet apart. He didn't look at her. Rather, it seemed he stared at nothing. Why did it feel as if she were under guard?

Gabriella fidgeted as she waited for Detective Arthur. She kept asking herself why someone could want Billy dead. What had he gotten into? Was it personal or work-related? Could it have something to do with what he discovered last night? But why would that get him killed?

And was she in danger now, too? She'd seen the likely killer, and he'd shot at her.

Just as fear threatened to unnerve her even more than before, Detective Arthur returned. He dismissed Officer Wilson with a nod and then sat beside her. "Are you ready to tell me what happened?"

She stared at him, and finally her throat opened to allow a simple question. "Why is Billy Holland dead?"

He'd shed his trench coat and hat, and even his necktie was askew, suit jacket unbuttoned. Somehow he seemed more trustworthy because of it. "Usually, our suspects would be the three women remaining at the house."

Her jaw opened, but no words emerged.

"But I don't believe that to be the case." He glanced at her. "Can you prove it to me by removing your coat?"

"My coat?" Gabriella looked down at her clothes. Her neck burned from the brick that had stung her there, but she wasn't hurt elsewhere. "Uh ... um ... what?"

Compassion flooded Detective Arthur's eyes, and he rested his hand on her arm. "Mr. Holland was shot, right?"

She shuddered but nodded. The image of his body rose in her mind. "Wait." She could see something just out of her grasp.

In a moment, she'd secured her pencil and drawing pad

from her satchel still hanging over her shoulder and flipped to a fresh page. Detective Arthur watched as the murder scene appeared on the blank sheet. Thankfully, he kept quiet as her pencil transcribed the image in her mind. The messy room, the bloodstains, the lifeless figure, even the bullet—

Gabriella jerked her gaze to Detective Arthur's. "He was shot in the back and up close. That's why the hole was so large and the smear on the floor from someone flipping him over. If I killed him, I'd have blood on my ... on my ... why is my head spinning?"

"Lean back, Miss Salatino." Detective Arthur took the pencil and pad from her, then helped her set her feet on the couch. "You've had a shock today. I'm going to have Officer Wilson take you home."

"You believe me?" Gabriella blinked away fresh tears. "I didn't kill Billy. He was my friend. My colleague. We were meeting to discuss our work over brunch before services."

Detective Arthur patted her shoulder like a father would. "I believe you, and I want to hear about that work, but later. I'll visit you this evening."

That would give her time to have Ali join them.

Six

Twenty minutes later, Gabriella and Officer Wilson climbed the steps to the Di Stasio building. The bells of St. Mark's across the street rang to signal the start of mass, leaving the street unnaturally quiet.

Usually she loved living so close to this particular Italian neighborhood. She could get Italian food that reminded her of her parents, and hear the language that had only been spoken at home. Her father had been the Heima Island lighthouse keeper, which is how a lone Italian family lived among so many blond-haired, blue-eyed people of nordic descent.

Now, however, she wished her fellow Italians weren't so dedicated to attending Mass. Then she wouldn't feel so vulnerable standing here alone with Officer Wilson. She wouldn't allow him inside, but would he force his way in? He still wore a mask-like expression that failed to hide his suspicion of her.

"Thank you for seeing me home." Gabriella rested her hand on the doorknob, but her cheeks heated at the gleam in his eye. Did he think she flirted with him? "You may go."

"I'd like to make sure your residence is secure, miss." Officer Wilson left no room for argument.

Secure? Did he think the murderer had come here?

So much for sending him away. Once inside, removed her coat as she waited for him to secure the downstairs kitchen, parlor, and office area. Lena hadn't returned yet either, as far as she could tell, and Ali rarely appeared on a Sunday.

When he returned to the foyer, Gabriella ducked her chin, adjusted the strap of her drawing satchel on her shoulder, and led the way up the steps. As they walked down the hallway to her rooms at the end, a chill ran down her spine. Ali insisted they lock their bedchamber doors since visitors frequented the downstairs. Now it stood ajar, just like Billy's had this morning.

Officer Wilson must have picked up on the fact that something was wrong, for he held out an arm, his other hand on his weapon. He gave her a look that said to stay put. She leaned against the wall between Carrie's and Emma's doors, willing her legs to hold her up, arms wrapped around herself. She could see her entire room from there, and the destruction left behind. Honestly, the only reason it didn't look as destroyed as Billy's room was because she had fewer things.

"Do you see anything missing?" Officer Wilson waved her inside.

She couldn't see anything, her sight blurred with frightened tears.

Officer Wilson raised his eyebrows, then sighed. "I need to contact Detective Arthur. Come with me."

Gabriella took one last look at the room. Committing it to memory to sketch later, watery as it all still looked. She had all her valuables, what few she had, on her person. She didn't have much.

Why was somebody doing this? What were they looking for that they'd tear apart a room like this? Why would someone want to target both of them? Did Billy surprise a thief and was murdered as a result? Or was the state of her apartment evidence that her life was now in danger, too? Could it be that attempting to meet Billy this morning saved her life?

Gabriella shuddered, blinking the tears out of her eyes, and Officer Wilson tucked her hand around his arm. Sturdy, comforting, but not entirely safe. Something protective had erased the suspicion that'd been in his expression a few moments ago.

"I-I need to call ..." Gabriella shook her head to jar loose the protocol for protecting Ali's identity, but explaining was harder than doing it herself.

Officer Wilson followed her to the telephone where she asked the operator to put her through to the extension of the fake solicitor's office. Gabriella didn't know the location of the building, just that it was kept occupied at all times and had access to runners who could deliver a message to Ali as quick as feet could carry them.

Message delivered, Officer Wilson led her to the parlor couch where he left her so he could call Detective Aurthur. She pulled out her sketch pad and let her pencil do its work. Something linked her and Billy. Could it be what they planned to discuss this morning? If so, what had Billy discovered?

Her questions were interrupted by the arrival of Ali and Detective Arthur. Ali was tiny, but her presence filled the room. The protests of the lawman bounced off her shoulders as she headed straight for Gabriella and pulled her into an embrace that belied her sixty-some years.

"I'm so sorry, *la mia stallina*." The Italian phrase that Ali called each of her journalists brought tears to

Gabriella's eyes. *My little star*. "Arthur is one of the good ones."

She didn't say Wilson was, but perhaps she hadn't had time to check. But knowing Arthur was an honorable cop eased part of Gabriella's worry.

"Miss Salatino and ..." Detective Arthur let the question of Ali's identity hang in the air.

Ali gave Gabriella one last squeeze, then turned to the detective with her hand extended sideways, like a businesswoman, not one of the elite ladies. "Alessandra Di Stasio. I own both the agency and the building. Miss Salatino is one of my journalists."

"A pleasure to make your acquaintance, Miss ... Di Stasio." Again, he hesitated and Gabriella hid a smile. The man was smart not to make assumptions about Ali. She had a way of making men realize women were their equal, with the same unalienable rights to life, liberty, and the pursuit of happiness.

"Now, where are you in the investigation?" Ali sat on the sofa beside her.

Detective Arthur shifted a high back chair so he could sit closer. He'd straightened his necktie since she'd seen him last, but his expression was much graver. "I believe the key to Mr. Holland's murder is the link between why he was attacked and why your rooms were searched."

Gabriella rubbed her thumb over the edge of her sketch, blurring the lines of her bedframe. "Do you think I could have been..."

"Killed, too?" Detective Arthur met Ali's eye for a brief moment. "As I told you, Miss Salatino, you would originally have been a prime suspect in Mr. Holland's murder. However, I had my doubts, as I told you, and now, either you're a stone cold killer who made it look like you're also a target, or, yes, I agree that someone wants you dead, too."

She felt blood drain from her body, as if that was possible. Did that happen to people? She half expected to see it pooling on the floor like it had under Billy. Her stomach turned. Ali didn't speak, just tightened her grip around Gabriella's shoulders.

"You and Holland worked together, correct?" Detective Arthur's question yanked her mind from the spiral in which it'd begun to descend. "For Miss Di Stasio?"

"Gabriella works for me, but Mr. Holland did not." Ali explained their connection and the temporary assignment to *Illinois Life Magazine*.

Detective Arthur wrote in his notebook, then looked at Gabriella. "Were you two friendly outside of the office?"

A little heat returned to her body. "We were friendly, but not an item, sir."

"Please do not sugarcoat or lie to me, Miss Salatino. It won't help me keep you alive."

Ali tensed beside her, giving her the gumption to answer for herself. "We were friendly. Nothing more."

He waited a beat, then tapped his notebook. "Is there anything particular that you and Mr. Holland were both working on that could be why you have been targeted?"

"Even when not working for *Illinois Life*, I cover charity events. That's why Billy and I knew one another. I'm not like my colleagues here. You've heard of C. C. Wagner?" She used Carrie's byline and it had the desired effect. The detective's eyes widened with respect. Gabriella shrugged. "Billy and I cover charity events, nothing that should get us..."

"Killed?" He scribbled in the notebook. "What were you working on?"

Ali rubbed a circle on Gabriella's back and she closed her notebook to hold it against her like a shield. "Last night, Billy and I attended a charity event at Susan and Charles Brink's estate for an article for his editor, Katherine Arkley. However, both Billy and I noticed that something was ... off. I didn't know what it was, so we agreed to meet for brunch this morning to talk about it. I remember everything I see and draw it, but I had the impression Billy knew something specific. I wish he'd been able to tell me what it was."

Detective Arthur slapped his notebook closed. "I don't like this, Miss Salatino. Is there someplace you can go where you'll be safe? With Miss Di Stasio, even. You cannot stay here, and I do not recommend anyone stay in this building until the culprit is found. I can also assign Officer Wilson to guard you both. He volunteered."

Of course he did. Gabriella frowned. She needed to talk this over with Ali without an audience.

"You can refuse our protection, Miss Salatino, but I don't think it wise."

"Might we discuss this in private, Detective Arthur?" Ali offered it as a question, but it wasn't.

Detective Arthur wisely left them alone.

"I'll telegraph Lena to extend her trip and the others will be away for a few days anyway." She tugged the drawing pad loose to hold Gabriella's hands. "But he's right, Gabriella. You cannot stay here. Not in this building and not in the city."

Gabriella's stomach twisted. "Where can I go?" Even as she asked the question, Andri came to mind. And home. Not that she had one on Heima Island anymore.

"*La mia stellina*, listen to me." Ali's accent thickened like it did when emotion grew. "You are right that you are not Carrie or Lena. They can handle powerful politicians and underhanded criminals. Even Emma has no fear of speaking to athletic men too full of themselves. But you, dear one, are beauty and art and have seen too much ugliness."

Tears pricked. "I can't turn a blind eye to injustice, Ali."

"This is why I'm glad you chose to join my agency. You are stronger than you realize. And I agree you have a gift God will use to unearth what others don't see because it comes in a pretty package. But, you cannot do that while looking over your shoulder. Look at yourself, Gabriella. You tremble unlike I have ever seen."

Not since Mama died had she felt this way.

"It is for both safety and healing that I send you away." Ali cupped her cheek like a mother would. "I know returning home is painful for you. I know you left your heart with a certain cop. This is the perfect opportunity to close that wound for good."

Gabriella stared. "How …"

"Come now, Gabriella." Ali grinned. "I'm a stunt reporter. I know all about you."

Which meant Chief Michelsen wasn't the only one who knew Gabriella had witnessed her mother's murder. Ali had found out. Somehow. And Gabriella shouldn't be surprised. That was Ali.

"Let Detective Arthur and me run our investigation,"

Ali continued, as if she hadn't revealed a secret, "and then you can return with your past fully behind you."

It had been seven years.

"Ladies?" Detective Arthur poked his head inside the parlor doors. "Do we have a decision? Officer Wilson can escort you."

"We do." Gabriella studied Ali's expression just to be sure. Her mentor, her boss, her friend, nodded. "I'll stay with a friend. He's a police officer on Heima Island, at the top of Door County in Wisconsin."

"Perfect. Well away from here." Detective Arthur tapped his fist on the side of the door. "Put me on the telephone with him, and I'll set up the details. Then Officer Wilson can drive you there as soon as you've packed your things."

"That won't be necessary." She did not want to be cooped up in an automobile with Officer Wilson for that many hours. Surely Ali had a contact who would be a much better option.

"It is, Miss Salatino. Officer Wilson will mind his manners and I'd prefer you have a police escort."

Ali placed a hand on Gabriella's forearm. "Please thank him for us."

"Ali," Gabriella hissed.

"Arthur is right," Ali said as the man slipped away. "You

need a police escort. Detective Arthur wouldn't send you with an officer he didn't trust to see you there safely."

Gabriella trusted Ali and Ali trusted Detective Arthur. That meant she did, too.

Even if it meant letting Officer Wilson drive her up to Heima Island so that Andri could protect her.

SEVEN

"WHAT IS SHE HIDING, Chief?" Andri tossed the cloth napkin onto his desk and leaned his chair back on its hind legs. Freya huffed beside him. She hated when he sat like this, especially when he had just finished eating—without giving her a bite. "Why didn't she want us to look in her cellar?"

"I agree that something fishy is going on." Michelsen replaced the empty bowls beside the soup crock in the basket his wife had brought over after services.

"With all due respect, sir, I can hear the *but*."

"But." Michelsen picked up Andri's napkin before dropping it and his own into the basket along with the utensils, then set the basket on the floor beside his desk. "Lydia Abrahams is one of the most outspoken supporters of the Eighteenth Amendment. Besides your father."

"That doesn't make her a saint." Andri dropped his chair back on all fours.

"Of course it doesn't." Michelsen glared at Andri. "But she cares about this town, as does your father. People like them keep this town protected from the inside. You and I keep it protected from the outside."

"We can't be effective at our job if people hide things."

"Lydia isn't just 'people,' Andri." Michelsen's sigh told him his mentor heard the pain behind Andri's statement. Ever since Gabby's mother was murdered, Andri had tried to get answers for her, only to be stonewalled. It'd sat in his craw like a burr and was part of the reason he'd turned to police work after getting his life back on the straight and narrow.

Freya rested her chin on his foot, and Andri rested his elbows on his knees, dropping his face into his hands.

"You've been on edge since last night, son." Michelsen's heavy steps stopped at the side of Andri's desk. "What's wrong with Gabby?"

A humorless laugh shot up his throat. "She needed a fake boyfriend last night. Over the telephone."

Silence, then the room erupted with Michelsen's hearty laughter. Andri scowled at him until the large man wiped at his eyes. "When will you come to your senses and call on her like she deserves?"

Andri clamped his lips shut. No one knew the real reason, and he'd sworn he would never tell.

Michelsen landed his large palm on Andri's equally large shoulder and brought the discussion back around to this morning's robbery. "You have a lot to learn about this job yet, Jóhannsson. One of those things is working within the hierarchy already in place. Just because you're the preacher's son doesn't mean you can walk over everyone as a policeman."

"I don't walk over people!" Andri shoved himself out of his chair. "But I am a policeman, and I don't like being left out of the information. There's something deeper going on than maintaining a dry community."

Michelson folded his hands, partially sitting on Andri's desk. "I know you mean well. Your exuberance is refreshing. But, Andri, take a breath. As policemen, we need cooperation. We can't bludgeon the truth out of people."

Andri opened his mouth to protest, but the chief held up a hand.

"Go home, Andri. Go see your family. It's Sunday. Tomorrow morning, we will begin digging. This is a long game, one we might not win, but we will try. Are you with me?"

Before Andri could reply, the office telephone rang. The chief answered, got an odd look on his face, then handed the candlestick phone to Andri and made himself conspicuously busy on the opposite side of the office.

"Hello?" He leaned his backside against the chief's desk.

"Andri?" Gabby. Something in her tone sounded ... tight, off, and definitely held more than her usual reservedness.

"What's wrong?" His heart rate kicked up. "Did that man from last night—"

"Detective Arthur would like a word."

Detective? Now she had his attention. And his concern. What had she gotten herself into?

"Officer Jóhannsson?" A gravely, male voice replaced Gabriella's.

Andri straightened from the desk, his gaze pinned to the chief's back. "This is Andri Jóhannsson. May I ask what's going on, sir?"

"I understand you are an officer with the Heima Island police?"

"Yes, sir."

"I understand you are acquainted with Miss Salatino." This wasn't a question as much as a vetting of him, as if the man could do that over a telephone line.

Andri braced his feet apart, the action causing Freya

to scramble to his side. "Sir, speak plainly. Is Gab—Miss Salatino in trouble?"

"There have been a few incidents today." Another law officer withholding information? Andri's anger spiked. "I'm sending Miss Salatino to Heima Island in order to stay under your protection."

"Protection? Incidents?" Andri snapped his fingers to get Michelson's attention, but the man stubbornly stayed on the opposite side of the room. "Is she okay?"

"She is physically unharmed, but I have reason to believe there is a threat on her life."

The words slammed into him, and he sank onto the chief's chair. Freya pressed against him. Gabby's mother had been his mother's best friend and the wife of the former lighthouse keeper, an Italian as gregarious as his booming laughter. The man had died performing a life-saving mission when Gabby was young, so Gabby and her mom moved next door to the Jóhannssons. Mrs. Salatino had been like a second mother to him and his sisters.

"Officer Jóhannsson?" The detective's sharp command pulled Andri from his thoughts long enough for another realization to hit him.

"The anniversary of Aunt Abigail's death. It was Thursday." As Andri spoke, Michelsen finally turned. No wonder his mother was so anxious about Tabby, who hadn't been at services this morning. "Detective Arthur, why is Gabby in mortal danger?"

"Jóhannsson, I believe you are the right man for this charge." Then he lowered his voice. "And I expect her person—and her heart—to be uninjured when I find the man who murdered her friend. Am I clear, officer?"

Andri stared at the phone in his hand as if the detective had jumped through the receiver. For some reason, this detective had taken on a fatherly role in protecting Gabby. From Andri, even while sending her here for him to guard. He searched for the chief, hoping for understanding, but the man had disappeared.

"Jóhannsson!" the detective barked. "Am I clear?"

"Yes, sir."

The answer jumped out, but Andri meant every syllable. He'd protected Gabby since they were kids, when his schoolmates teased her and other girls picked on her for looking so different. Then in the years since that fateful day when he made the biggest mistake of his life, he'd mastered protecting her from himself.

However, that task, even from a distance, took its toll on him. Up close? When he had to physically protect her? Share space with her? He could and would do the job, but it would likely decimate his heart in the process.

EIGHT

Andri crooked his neck to see the clock as he stirred the pot stew his mother had sent home with him. The last ferry of the day had crossed when the sun went down hours ago, but the chief had made special arrangements with a few locals, including having one of the few automobiles on the island—a farm truck—available to transport Gabby from the fisherman's boat to Andri's home.

He stoked the fire to keep the meal warm. The hours of waiting had been torture and yet it felt like each second counted down to his doom. Gabriella was a ... unique girl. Woman. Gabby and Ruthie were fast friends, so Ruthie kept tabs on her since Andri had caused her to flee Heima Island. At least she still called Andri when she was in trouble.

Freya jumped to her feet as the sound of automobile tires crunched in the yard. She didn't charge the door, but her muscles tensed as she kept all her focus on Andri.

"It's alright, girl." Andri snagged his lantern and patted her head. "They're friendlies."

Freya's tail gave a small wag, then she followed him to the front porch. Headlights punched through the darkness, illuminating Andri and Freya without need for his measly light. He hung it on the porch hook anyway. Electricity had not made it to the island yet, but talk was the lighthouse would get it soon.

The truck engine stayed running as a man in uniform emerged from the driver's side. Andri rested his hands on his belt, and Freya sat at his side while they waited on the porch.

"Officer Andri Jóhannsson?" The cop kept his distance, his breath a white puff in the cold air.

The passenger side door flung open and Gabby popped out wearing a dark wool coat. "*Mamma mia*, stop this formality. Officer Wilson, Andri will take care of me."

Andri's chest expanded at her confidence in him.

"It's too improper, Gabriella." Wilson slammed his door and walked to Gabriella's side of the car. Freya stood. "You told me he is not married."

They talked about him? Wait, why had the officer used Gabby's first name? The man was correct, though, it would be too improper for Gabby to stay here without a chaperone. But Andri already had a plan for that.

Gabby slung first the strap of one bag, then another over her shoulder. "I'm going over to Ruthie's. Not that it is any of your concern." Did Gabby's voice shake?

"I can't let you do that, Gabriella." The cop grabbed her bicep, forced her to stop. Her free hand came up and would have slapped him if he hadn't blocked it.

Anger flashed through Andri and he bounded down the steps. Freya leaped ahead with a menacing growl.

Gabby cried out. Wilson's gun cleared its holster aiming at Freya, but Freya had shoved herself between the gun and Gabby, severing Wilson's hold on her, and Wilson had lowered his weapon, all before Andri managed to reach them.

"Make the dog stand down." Wilson glared at Freya.

Freya leaned closer to Gabby, forcing her to take a step away from the officer.

Andri breathed out the bite he wanted to put in his words. "You are relieved, Officer Wilson. Freya and I will see to Miss Salatino's protection."

Wilson holstered his weapon and folded his arms, but Andri had five inches on the man and was not intimidated.

Not that Wilson was short: he towered over Gabby's diminutive frame, a form made smaller as she hugged her arms around her slim waist.

"Andri?" Yes, her voice did shake. Her knit cap held her black curls close around cheeks made pale in the headlights.

"You have a truck to return and a ferry to catch, Officer Wilson." Andri moved to put himself between the cop and Gabby. A man needn't be in uniform to portray the authority of an officer.

Wilson peered around Andri. "I can't force you, Gabriella, but is this what you want?"

Gabby must have nodded because Wilson shot Andri a murderous look, then got in the truck and drove away, taking the light with him.

"Andri?" Her hand touched his back.

He turned and took in his first good look at the girl he hadn't seen in seven years. Not girl. Woman. Round cheeks and narrow chin filled a face that tucked perfectly into his shoulder. He knew because he'd held her all those years ago, when her mama died.

The lighthouse beam flashed over their heads, reflecting the fear in her eyes. And the consternation. He'd always liked that about her. She could hold two conflicting emotions simultaneously.

She stepped back, woolen skirt swishing around her knees. "Now what?"

Andri swallowed past the sand gathering in his throat. "Come inside. I'll call my mother. She has a plan."

Gabby eased into the lantern light with Freya attached to her leg. Andri tried not to stare, but Gabriella Salatino stood on his porch looking as gorgeous, and as vulnerable, as the last day he'd seen her, the satchels weighing—

Satchels! What an obtuse man he was!

"Can I take those?" He pointed to the bags he should have asked to take minutes ago.

She caught her lip in her teeth and Andri had to fight the urge to wrap her in a hug. No woman had ever made him feel as protective as she did. But that had been his downfall after her mother died.

"It's too cold and dark to be out here." He took the bags and opened the door for her to urge her inside.

The warmth from his stove greeted them as they entered the kitchen. Gabby shivered. "Thank you for sending Officer Wilson on his way. He is rather boorish, but Detective Arthur trusts him."

Andri's brows slammed down before he could stop them. "Did he make you uncomfortable?"

Gabriella nodded and her cheeks flamed a deep auburn. "Thank you for always being my scapegoat ... friend."

He couldn't keep from touching her. His hand dwarfed her shoulder, but her cheek inclined toward it, so he left it there rather than removing it. "I'm sorry for everything that has happened, Gabby, but it's good to see you." *After all these years.*

She met his gaze with one filled with a thousand questions. Oh yeah, he'd missed her. They—with his sister Ruthie—had been an inseparable trio. Until …

He shook away the past and helped her out of her coat. "Mother left us stew until she could come over. Chief Michelsen will want to hear everything, too. But Gabby, what's going on? You witnessed a murder? You're in danger?"

Her shoulders dropped and he clenched his teeth. He hadn't meant to level her with questions, at least not so soon. He'd lectured himself all afternoon to go easy on her, to not let emotion get the best of him. Again.

"I'm sorry." He hung her coat on the rack, set her satchels in his spare room, then escaped to the stove, not trusting the words that could come out of his mouth. Or worse, the ridiculous wish to comfort her.

"I didn't mean to get into this mess." She followed him, her voice quiet. "I don't mean to impose either, and Officer Wilson was right about it not being good for me to stay here alone with you."

Andri flinched. "I wouldn't—" *take advantage of you*.

"Of course not. I'm like your little sister." She carried the filled bowls to the table while he gathered two mugs to hide his reaction to her words. "But I refuse to bring harm to Ruthie's home, especially not with her expecting a baby. Heaven forbid the man follows me here. What if he comes after me? Andri, I can't believe this is happening again."

Andri was by her side before Freya this time and he tossed caution to the wind as he pulled her into his arms.

The years melted away and he was transported to the last time he'd held her. They'd been kids, really, on the verge of adulthood and with a lack of maturity to match. They'd just laid her mother to rest, and he'd held her as she cried. Then she kissed him.

And he'd been too shocked to return it before their friendship fractured.

She pushed away from him now, spinning in a slow circle as if looking for her mooring. "I can go to the chief's house. Why I didn't think of that before, I—"

"Gabby." He stopped her movement and directed her to sit. "You're staying here."

He and Michelsen had already agreed it was the safest option. Being on the edge of town where few would even know Gabby had returned made it the wisest choice. She glared at him with such a mixture of independence and fear that he worried his self-control would falter and he'd kiss her like he should have done that afternoon in the graveyard. But now wasn't the time.

Anger at himself for these ridiculous emotions had him growling at her. "Eat the stew and if I catch you outside before I get back, I'll throw you in jail myself. Is that clear?"

She crossed her arms. "You always were so full of yourself."

He couldn't deny that it used to be true. "Freya, stay."

With a slam, he yanked the front door closed behind him as he left the house. He had to get out of there before he said—or did—something else he'd regret.

NINE

GABRIELLA SANK BACK INTO the chair, eyes closed. What was it about Andri that made emotion churn like a cauldron in her chest? Freya rested her head in Gabriella's lap, demanding that she pet her.

"You're a sweet girl." Gabriella rubbed the bridge of Freya's long snout. "Protective. Like your master."

When her father moved their family to the island, Gabriella found in Ruthie her missing half. Though opposite in every way, the townspeople called them the Lighthouse Twins because that's usually where they played. Two years older, Andri would grudgingly tag along to keep an eye on them, as his parents instructed.

Somewhere along the way, the grumbling turned from real to pretend and they became a trio. As they grew older,

Ruthie knew Gabriella harbored a crush on her older brother. In fact, she often tried to manufacture ways to get the two of them alone together, which would only backfire. Andri would end up yelling at his sister and Gabriella would melt into a puddle of embarrassment.

Gabriella knew Andri only saw her as another sister, and loved her as a brother would. She knew that's why he'd held her after her mother died, why he held her tonight. But just like then, she didn't feel sisterly toward him.

"Freya, what am I going to do?" Gabriella rested her forehead against the dog's. "There is a reason I stayed away all these years."

A wet nose nudged her chin and Gabriella chuckled, inhaling the scent of beef and vegetables. Aunt Deborah Jóhannsson made the best stew. Not once had Gabriella had its match. Freya sat as Gabriella spooned a bite, the dog's soulful eyes following every moment.

Gabriella raised a brow. "You can't have any unless Andri says so."

Freya's tale thumped.

As she ate, Gabriella allowed her attention to leave the dog and travel through Andri's home. Ruth had told her he'd built it himself a couple years ago. It suited him. Rough hewn walls. Main floor with an attic. Braided rugs she'd guess were from his mother or sister. The mantle had only a family portrait, taken before Ruth's youngest was born two years ago. There had once been a day when she was considered part of the family, she and her mom. Then she'd allowed grief to override her good sense and ruined everything.

Freya bumped Gabriella's hand with her head, insisting on a pat. "That's probably why he ran out of here, huh? He was afraid I'd kiss him again."

History will not repeat itself.

Tears pricked her eyes. She didn't regret her decision to leave Heima Island, but she missed the safety she used to feel. Missed feeling close to a family, even if they weren't hers by blood. Ali offered the motherliness Gabriella missed, but with her colleagues always off tracking down a story, Gabriella felt alone more often than not.

She pushed the bowl of stew toward the center of the table, her appetite gone. Maybe agreeing to come to the island was a bad idea. But being protected by someone like Officer Wilson was worse. She shuddered. The man might be an honorable cop, and he hadn't crossed a professional line, but he'd wanted to get to know her and kept hinting on asking her out after the case was solved. Talk of Andri proved a natural buffer.

"Freya, I have to help somehow. I have to find a way to bring this to a swift conclusion." For all their sakes.

Even Ali didn't think she had what it took to be an investigative journalist like Carrie or Lena, and perhaps she was right. Gabriella had never been able to help solve her mother's murder. Her resolve strengthened. She couldn't let that happen again. Something got Billy killed.

She scratched Freya's ears. "But what was the murderer looking for? Why kill Billy? And what does it have to do with me?"

Freya answered by trotting to the door. Gabriella glanced over her shoulder as Andri ducked to enter. Her face heated as she watched him slowly close the door against the chilly March night. She remembered when he was a lanky boy, always taller than her, of course. But at some point, she had stopped growing and he had kept reaching for the sky.

He shrugged out of his winter coat, muscles rippling across a cotton shirt that stretched tight across his back, and removed his hat. He'd filled out since she'd last seen him. Turned from the brink of manhood into ... well, a very good-looking man. He had grown more handsome in the years she'd been away. The white-blond hair he'd had as a youth was now streaked with red. Her sketches had not done him justice.

"I'm not going to turn into a bear, Gabby." Humor wrapped around his words.

Embarrassment captured her tongue, and she covered her flaming face, watching him approach through her fingers. Silent as a panther, even with his size, he walked with purpose, yet slowed as he grew near. Freya trotted behind him, watchful, as if not sure who needed her most, her master, or her visitor. Then he stopped beside her, and kneeled, bringing his brilliant blue eyes nearly level with hers. Gabriella's breath stalled in her lungs, and her hands dropped to her lap.

"Gabby." He rested a hand on the back of her chair. "I'm sorry for leaving you. I should have exercised more self-restraint. Will you forgive me?"

Gabriella gaped at him, unsure what to say. She hadn't expected an apology. Andri had done nothing wrong. She was the one who'd showed up unexpectedly, who, once again, thrown herself at him. The annoying little sister with the equally annoying crush.

"Hey." His rough fingers touched her chin when she tried to hide the emotions surely swirling in her eyes. "Can we begin again?"

She nodded, not sure what else to say except ... "I'm not sure how long I'll be here and I do not want to inconvenience you. But thank you for taking me in. I'm not sure where else I would have gone. And, well, I've ... I've missed you." She squeezed her eyes and lips shut to prevent more unauthorized words from spilling out.

Andri's chuckle rumbled. "I've missed you, too, Gabby. Can you look at me?"

Gabriella pried her lids open to find Andri's expression one of compassion, though he'd shifted away from her.

"We'll find our footing again, no matter how long or short you need to stay here." He awkwardly patted her knee. "And I will protect you. You know that right?"

"I do. That's why I always come running to you, even if it's over the phone." Gabriella covered her face with her hands as the truth slipped out once again. "I'm sorry, Andri. I'm tired and scared and words just keep escaping me."

Whether she wanted Andri to know all of that or not, the words were out. And like that day when she'd kissed him, her brain caught up too late.

"Gabby." His palm brushed her hair as if she were a child and emotion balled in her chest.

"This is why I prefer my pencil and drawing pad," she muttered. Frustration pushed her to her feet. If only the proverbial cat would keep hold of her tongue. "I don't make mistakes when I draw, or say things I'm not supposed to say."

"Oh, Gabby." Andri laughed as he stood. "How much have you eaten?"

"Of your mother's stew? Only a bite or two." The change of topic spun her toward him and loosed an idea that would change this unwieldy topic. "Andri, your house has need of art. So, to thank you for being my escape from Officer Wilson, I am going to draw you something. I'll even add some color to it if you want; I have colored pencils. A sketch is like a memory, so, I am going to leave you with multiple memories that you can put on your walls so that this rustic cabin of yours will look more like a home. And, *mamma mia*, I'm going to stop talking now."

Andri rested his hands on his belt with a wink. "I think that is exactly what my walls need."

Gabriella escaped to the washbasin. Though unsure what to do with her uneaten food, she was desperate to get a handle on her roiling emotions. "You said your mom has a plan for me? Would I be able to learn what it is?"

Andri jabbed his thumb at the telephone box on his kitchen wall. "I'll call her so she knows you've arrived. For tonight, she is going to stay in my room and I'll make a pallet on the floor in front of the stove with Freya. Then tomorrow we will figure out how we're going to make this work. Okay?"

Freya's tail wagged at the mention of her name. Gabriella reached for the dog so she didn't have to look at Andri. "I don't want to displace you. Look at what inconvenience I'm causing. You are going to sleep on the floor, your mother is not going to sleep in her home, and ... and ... and ..."

"Gabby. It's okay. I am glad you are here. It would kill me if something happened to you because I couldn't stop it."

That brought Gabriella's gaze up.

Andri's face had turned bright red to match the streaks in his hair and he backed away. "Fine. That's the truth, Gabby. You might as well hear it. Every time you called it would make me feel better that at least I could do *something*."

He felt that way? Gabriella stared at him. She always thought Andri was annoyed when she called for his help. But she always felt safer when she called him, always felt better. Knowing now that he appreciated that she called him? It hurt even as it warmed her.

"I know you initiated that .... no." He shook his head and backed up still further.

Gabriella's heart stuttered. Was he about to bring up her kiss?

"You know what, never mind." Andri stomped to the telephone box and relief whooshed out of Gabriella. She wasn't ready to talk about it. "We are not going to worry about what the past has been or where it has brought us. I'm going to keep you safe and we're going to let detective Arthur do his job and figure out who killed your colleague."

She relaxed for the first time that day, it seemed. Andri's discomfiture gave her a feeling of camaraderie that put them back on level ground. This giant of a man wasn't as put together as he liked people to think. Or maybe she just had that effect on him? Like a mouse to an elephant. The thought widened her smile. Yes, if they could settle into the teasing of a big brother and little sister, perhaps they could get through this without heartache.

Her cheer dipped. She doubted she'd ever be able to see him that way again. But perhaps, this time, when she left Heima Island, she could leave her childhood feelings behind.

TEN

THE FOLLOWING MORNING, ANDRI escaped his house for his morning run, leaving his mother to look after Gabby. He jogged along the coast with Freya by his side and his breath puffed out in tiny white clouds. The bright blue sky above allowed the sun to shine, with the slightest hint of warmth. Winter wasn't keen on giving up its grip, but the sun would win ... eventually.

With only two policemen on the island, he and Chief Michelsen split morning duties. Andri would jog the perimeter of the island, and the chief would visit the shops as they opened and converse with residents along the way.

Heima Island took up about five hundred acres between Lake Michigan and Green Bay. Though larger than Plum Island across Death's Door, it was smaller than

Washington Island to the north. Its three miles of coast equaled the perfect run, though today he ran those miles faster than usual before detouring to Ruthie's house.

"Uncle Andri!" Seven-year-old Seve, Ruthie's eldest, launched himself out of the back door and into Andri's arms, heedless of the chill weather. Seve's two-year-old brother, Jack, ran after him. The boys' blond-hair and blue eyes looked so much like the Jóhannsson side of the family, he sometimes forgot they were also Nilsson boys.

"Hiya!" Andri tipped Seve upside down, holding him by his feet. "Got anything in those pockets?"

Seve belly laughed.

Freya's tail wagged her hindquarters as Jack wrapped his chubby arms around her neck; she had a special relationship with Andri's nephews, especially Jack. She ran her long tongue over Jack's dirty face, effectively wiping breakfast off his chin.

Still giggling, Seve freed his feet from Andri's grasp and rolled to the ground. "This is funner than school," he said, except it sounded like *thith ith funner than thool* because the kid had lost both front teeth last week.

"You're about the only one who can drag the boys away from pancakes." Ruthie pushed through the screen door, five-year-old Teddy following with his arm around her leg. "Boys, your pancakes are getting cold."

"Okay!" Seve dashed inside, nearly knocking Teddy over in his haste.

"Doggy, too?" Jack had his fingers wrapped in her fur.

"Go on." Andri nodded to Freya and the dog trotted after Jack.

"Shouldn't you be home with Ma and Gabby?" Ruthie rubbed her pregnant belly, then waved him into the warmth of her kitchen.

Andri swung Teddy away from his mama. "These boys get bigger by the minute."

"It runs in the family." Ruthie's indulgent smile warmed him. She might be his younger sister, but she had enough maternal instinct to include him as one of her boys.

Andri tickled Teddy's chin, sending the boy into giggles. Teddy was the quietest of his nephews, but his laughter wrapped around Andri's chest and eased the tension in his shoulders.

Of course, Ruthie noticed. "Is it the guilt you refuse to acknowledge, or the danger she's facing?"

Andri ignored that question, too, as he plunked Teddy into his chair, a plate of half-eaten pancakes before him. It may have been a miscalculation on his part to stop by Ruthie's this morning, but seeing his nephews always made his day brighter.

"I have a spelling bee today," Seve said around the bite of a pancake smothered in maple syrup from the peninsula.

"Oh yeah?" Andri sat beside Jack and tore pancakes into bite size pieces for him.

Seve nodded. "Beth beat me last time. She always spells faster than I do, but I practiced a lot this time."

"Plate." Ruthie set one in front of Andri. "More pancakes are on the way."

"I don't—" He stopped the words at his sister's raised brow. Yeah, yeah, he should know by now that Ruthie hated being babied when she was expecting one. He couldn't help himself, though. She was his little sister.

"Teddy is reading real good." Seve plopped another pancake on his plate. "You should hear him read the primer."

"Oh?" Andri winked at his middle nephew. "That means you can read me a bedtime story."

Teddy's round face turned as red as the streaks in his white-blond hair.

"Finish up." Ruthie set another stack of pancakes in the middle of the table. "You two need to leave for school in ten minutes."

Andri plated four pancakes. "I can walk them over."

Ruthie narrowed her gaze at him and he shoved a large bite in his mouth. The schoolhouse was only three blocks away and the children had to pass city hall, where Ruthie's husband had his office, in order to get there.

Seve cleared his plate then leapt to his feet. "C'mon, Ted. Race you."

Teddy shoved away from the table.

"Don't forget your coats and lunch pails," Ruthie called above the ruckus.

"Yes, ma'am!" Seve answered for both boys.

"And hug your mother." Andri waved his fork at them.

Hugs given, winter clothes donned, lunchpails and school books secured, the two boys ran out the door.

The room grew awkwardly silent, and Andri knew Ruthie had something to say. He focused on Jack, who was threatening to fling pancake chunks across the table. "Why don't you spit out what you want to tell me?"

Ruthie turned from the stove and wagged the spatula at him. "When are you going to talk to her? Really talk."

Andri glared at her.

Ruthie glared back. "I don't know what went wrong, what sent both of you running from the Island. She won't tell me, and heaven knows you never will. But I want to whack both of you upside the head and tell you to finally talk about it. I want my brother and my sister-of-the-heart both at supper with me, together, without the air crackling like a thunderstorm."

He should have known he wouldn't be able to hide his angst around his sister. He'd stayed away whenever Gabriella made a rare visit, which was only to meet the newest members of the family as they arrived.

Andri crossed his arms. Trouble was, he knew he should have talked with Gabby years ago. But admitting to his mistake? "I'm a prideful man, Ruthie. You'd think God would have taught me humility by now." Dare he ask God for such a painful lesson?

Ruthie's gaze softened and she rested her long fingers on his biceps. "God must have had other lessons for you to learn first, brother dearest."

Jack babbled around a bite of pancake.

Andri kept his focus on his nephew. "It's my fault she's stayed away."

Ruthie hummed and rubbed her belly with her spare hand. "You need to forgive yourself. The actions she took after she left are not your fault."

Andri opened his mouth to protest when Jack lobbed a smashed bit of pancake at his face. It splattered on his cheek, rolled down his chin, and landed on the floor.

Ruthie laughed. "Freya, clean up after your cousin and father, would you?"

Father. Andri's heart twisted. He'd always wanted to be one, but that required a wife. Oh sure, he'd called on a few women during his wilder days on the peninsula. While he didn't cross any lines that his conscience wouldn't allow, he didn't treat them with the respect they deserved either. They were an escape, a self-inflicted punishment, for sending his sister's best friend running from home.

He gave Freya a hand signal indicating she could eat the pancake. Freya scrambled for the morsel and Jack tossed her another one. She didn't wait for permission this time. Andri rolled his eyes. Freya refused food from everyone unless Andri gave permission, except Jack. Neither boy nor dog cared whether they were allowed to share or not.

Ruthie swept the remaining pieces of pancake into her hand and Andri set Jack on the ground to play with Freya. Before he left, he needed to ask if Ruthie had talked to their baby sister. Ma insisted he have a chat with Tabby when she returned from working at Kristiansen's today. But if he steered their conversation away from Gabby too soon, he'd pay for it.

So, he waited for his dog to herd his nephew toward the warmth of the stove, always keeping her body between the danger and her charge, before emitting a heavy sigh meant to get his sister's attention. "Promise me you'll leave the topic alone when you talk with Gabby? I need to focus on keeping her alive, not having you play peacemaker."

"Will you promise to talk with her?" Ruthie cleared the

rest of the table.

Refusing his sister would amount to giving her the go-ahead to talk to Gabby. "She's in danger, Ruthie. Maybe once this is all over, she and I can talk, but for now, I'm asking you to leave it alone. Please."

Ruthie failed to turn away from him before surprise flashed across her pale features. She continued to turn a full circle before pinning him with her motherly gaze. "For now, Brother. For now."

It was the best he could hope for. "Now, about Tabby. Why is Ma so worried?"

Eleven

Gabriella woke to the smell of bacon and coffee and ... fresh bread? Aunt Deborah had been busy this morning while Gabriella lollygagged in bed. She dressed quickly despite stiff muscles, gathered her drawing pad and pencil, and emerged from the room Andri had given her to sleep in. Her traitorous heart gave a leap at the possibility of seeing Andri, only to find the thin woman humming by his stove was alone.

It shouldn't hurt that Andri wasn't here to greet her, but why wouldn't he be here to protect her? Maybe he thought she deserved the mess she was in? No, no, he'd made it clear yesterday he liked when she called him for help, and he always made her feel safe.

Equilibrium regained, Gabriella cleared her throat so

she wouldn't startle Andri's mother.

"Morning, sweet one." Aunt Deb turned from the stove with a smile. "Andri had patrol this morning, but promised to return as soon as he could. I wouldn't be surprised to see him appear as soon as the bacon is finished cooking."

Gabriella chuckled and she set her drawing pad on the table. "It smells delicious. May I help?"

As she expected, Aunt Deb waved away the question. "Perhaps tomorrow. Today you are a guest. And a long-lost guest." She raised an eyebrow as Gabriella sat at the table, one leg tucked under her navy wool skirt.

Aunt Deb hadn't pestered her with questions after she arrived last night, though Gabriella had fallen asleep to her and Andri's whispered conversation. Were they discussing her? For once, she wouldn't let curiosity kill her.

She flipped open her drawing pad and assessed her mother's friend. Would Aunt Deb turn grey? Her hair was already so blonde it appeared white. Like her daughters. Andri, too, except he had streaks of red …

Gabriella's gaze shot up as she realized she'd completely forgotten to answer Andri's mother. But what had she asked? What were they talking about? "Sorry, Aunt Deb, what was the question?"

Aunt Deb stepped away from the stove with a frown. "I

didn't ask one. Are you sure you're all right, sweetie? I have no need to pry, but I know you're in some kind of trouble. Andri is a good man—of course I'm biased—but you can trust him to do right by you."

Gabriella flushed. What kind of trouble did she think Gabriella was in? "It's a police matter, Aunt Deb."

Aunt Deb pursed her lips and Gabriella flipped her drawing pad to a fresh sheet, not knowing what else to say to the woman who was like a second mother. But it seemed to be enough for her, and she returned to the stove and let Gabriella draw.

Most mornings, Gabriella began with a blank page, letting her mind empty itself of whatever she couldn't quite grasp. Sometimes she'd draw her parents, other times Ruthie, even Andri, but most times her scenes were of something that happened the day or two before.

Such was the case this morning.

As Aunt Deb placed a mug of coffee near Gabriella's left hand, a scene unfolded under the pencil she held in her right. Not just any scene ... the scene of Billy's murder.

Andri's kitchen disappeared as the image in Gabriella's mind appeared on the page before her. Whoever murdered Billy must have been looking for something. But if it had been papers, the mess would have been focused on the desk. If it was his journalist notebook, why toss the rest of the room? Why rip open cushions? Why empty the wardrobe?

Why go to her place after killing Billy?

Heartache squeezed in her chest. Had she gotten Billy killed?

A thought for later. After she helped the police solve this ... this ... *Mamma mia*, she was missing something. What?

She tapped her fingers on the table, then switched to a new page. Under her pencil appeared page notes from her desk. She and Billy only had a few open stories they shared.

Why did people like having a window into the way the wealthy lived? She felt as if the elegant galas captured the wealthy in a fish bowl. What a thought! She turned to a new page and drew a scene from Saturday's gala, but in a fish bowl.

The faces of Susan and her husband, Thomas Cook, George Zander and his daughter appeared under her pencil. Elegance. Extravagance. Ev—

"What are you drawing?" Andri appeared behind her shoulder.

Gabriella screamed, her pencil flying into the air.

Andri towered above her, a giant of Norse descent, with a ferocious scowl. "I've been talking for the last three minutes."

Gabriella's heart pounded and Freya shoved her furry

face under Gabriella's trembling hands. "I ... I didn't hear you."

Andri was supposed to be a tower of strength, not fear. She curled her fingers into Freya's fur. Why couldn't she stop shaking? Why were tears spearing her eyes?

She jumped with a squeak when Andri touched her shoulder. "I didn't mean to scare you, Gabby. I'm sorry."

Gabriella nodded, hoping that would be enough to stop his questions. She had no answers to give. Thankfully, Andri didn't speak, though he never looked away from her as he took the chair kitty-corner.

"Sit and eat." Aunt Deb set a plate of bacon, toast, and scrambled eggs in front of both of them. "I need to check on your father. Come by for supper tonight and I'll walk back with you."

"I can't ask you to do that." Gabriella blinked back the tears. She was disrupting lives all over again. But what choice did she have? Return home where her room had been ransacked? Stay alone with Andri and ruin their reputations? *He'll do right by you.* "I can stay with you instead, Aunt Deb."

The older woman shook her head. "We have a family staying with us right now. They lost their home to the bank just after the new year. The husband is looking for work on the mainland, but hasn't found anything yet."

Gabriella dropped her chin. "Then I can't stay with you any more than I can stay at Ruthie's. It's too dangerous." Why had Ali thought this the perfect solution? *It is for both safety and healing that I send you away.*

Aunt Deb pulled Gabriella into a hug. "It's also why I can stay here. Mrs. Berg is tending to my house while I am here. So, don't you fret about anything. You're family and family helps one another."

She swallowed a sob. "Thanks, Aunt Deb."

"Now eat up, both of you." Aunt Deb pointed a finger at Andri, then Gabriella. "I'll see you at supper."

"Yes, ma'am." Andri rose. "I'll see you out."

Andri's momentary absence—and Freya's, since the dog followed her master to the door—gave Gabriella a moment to collect herself. It felt as if her world spun, leaving her unsure of her footing. She hadn't felt so disoriented since her mamma died. Then she'd kissed Andri and everything had fallen apart.

She couldn't let that happen again. She wouldn't. Ali was right, she could use this time to heal from the past, to move on, become stronger. She might wield a drawing pencil instead of a typewriter, but she could be an investigative journalist just like her colleagues. Like Billy, too. The social elite hide criminal behavior and she could ferret it out using her illustrations.

With newfound determination, she returned to her chair and nibbled a bite of bacon as she studied the fish bowl image. What were these wealthy men up to?

"I don't like that look on your face, Gabby." His chair creaked as Andri lowered his frame into it. "You aren't investigating your colleague's murder."

Gabriella ignored his directive. "My meeting with Billy was to discuss ... someone. Could that have gotten Billy killed?" Or had someone seen her and Billy on their date the previous week? She'd heard of people killed out of jealousy, but who would have that type of obsession with her?

She shuddered. Thomas Cook.

But no. He wouldn't kill and ransack, would he? But he could hire someone. Someone who could just as easily follow her to Heima Island. If Mr. Cook saw her with Andri, would Andri be in danger if she stayed?

"Gabby?" Andri's quiet voice, then the gentle touch he laid on her arm drew her from her churning thoughts with the promise of comfort. "You turned white as a sheet. What just went through your mind?"

Words spilled out at the compassion in Andri's blue eyes. "What if I brought danger to the island? What if a murderer followed me? If your mother, or Ruthie, or the boys are in danger because of me, I'll never forgive myself."

Andri's large fingers wrapped around her hand. "I'm well-aware you might have danger following. That's exactly why you're here. Gabby, I will keep you safe."

"I know you will." But at what cost? Gabriella set her jaw. Andri was a real-life hero any girl would swoon over. *Which is why I kissed him.* Not this time. Ali sent her here to heal, not repeat the past. Now she would keep *him* safe.

From herself.

And the trouble she knew nipped at her heels.

TWELVE

ANDRI WATCHED THE CHANGE come over Gabby's features. One moment, vulnerability covered her like a cloak, the next she turned resolute. While the former was more dangerous to his heart, the latter worried him most.

To buy himself a moment to think, Andri gathered the dishes to return to the wash basin. Gabby closed her sketch pad and disappeared into the guest room, leaving Andri alone with his thoughts. Even Freya followed her.

Andri pumped water into the basin and scrubbed the bacon grease from the plates. His preference would be to leave her at the house, but not alone. Not only would he worry for her safety, it concerned him, what he'd seen in her notebook. He'd gotten a good glimpse before she realized he'd been watching her.

He thought she'd known he'd returned, that the bouncing of her head had been a nod of greeting. He had even carried on a conversation with his mother about how many pieces of bacon he wanted—of course she'd made double that amount—and still Gabby had drawn in her notebook. Andri rested his forearms on the washbasin's edge. That fishbowl. Filled with dressed-up people. Men of wealth. It shouldn't have spiked a sense of jealousy in him. This was the world she lived in, the world she worked in.

Andri sighed. Ruthie subscribed to the magazines that featured Gabby's work the most and left them on the table for Tabby to read. He read them, too, though neither he nor Ruthie acknowledged the fact. He hefted the washbasin, opened the back door, and flung the water well away from the walkway.

Freya trotted toward him. He scratched her ears after he replaced the washbasin. He could hear Gabby moving around in the other room and despised the cozy sense her presence brought to his home. It reminded him of his failure. Had he been mature enough all those years ago, perhaps they could have had a future together.

Instead, he had hurt her. Driven her away from those who loved her just when she had lost the most. Now he could offer nothing except his protection, and so, when he had interrupted her drawing, the fear that flashed in her eyes speared a harpoon straight through his gut.

"Andri?" Gabby emerged from her room wearing her wool coat, a hat, and mittens. "The way I see it, you can either leave me here or I can join you at the station. I would like the opportunity to say hello to Chief Michelsen. Is ... is that alright with you?"

Andri fisted his hand at the slip of her bravado. He'd scared her even worse than he thought.

She kept her eyes averted as she placed her drawing pad in the smaller of her satchels. "If it's more convenient, I can walk to the station myself. It's not far. There are plenty of people around. I'm sure I will be just fine."

"Gabby." He measured his steps as he approached. Here on the island, surrounded by other men of Nordic descent, he was brawny. But to Gabby? He hadn't realized how much larger he must appear to her until today.

Freya sat on Gabby's foot, keeping her attention.

"Yours is a good idea." He paused a foot away from her.

She was correct that he could not leave her at his pregnant sister's home nor could he leave her with his mother where she would be surrounded by young children.

"I promised you safety, Gabby." His words had their

desired effect when she raised her brown eyes. "I have no doubt the island is the best place for you to be, the safest place. Can you trust me to protect you?"

Something flashed in her eyes that twisted something within his chest. A lot of something he didn't understand. Nor did he know how he could do his job keeping an island safe while also keeping her safe. But he would, even if it came at great cost to his peace of mind. Because having Gabby in his work domain would certainly be a distraction he couldn't afford.

"Come on." He flung his arm over her shoulders the way he had as a youth, the familiar action settling him. "The chief is looking forward to seeing you."

Bundled against the cold, they followed the mile-long path to the police station. Gabby walked silently on his left, Freya between them. Andri rarely wore a holstered weapon on the Island, so it felt odd tucked under his left arm. The crime they policed wasn't criminal as much as it was peace-keeping. Which made the smugglers last night more worrisome.

Then there was Gabby. He wanted to keep her away from trouble, from investigating, not bring her into the heart of an active investigation, especially one that involved the illegal sale and distribution of alcohol.

The Volstead Act had been in effect since '20, but

Wisconsin stopped enforcing it at the state level in the middle of last decade, and two years ago repealed all state prohibition laws, leaving it to the Feds or the local cops to enforce. Heima Island, being a dry town since before the Noble Experiment began, meant Andri and Chief Michelsen were left to enforce it within their few square miles.

"I don't remember it being this cold in March." Gabby popped the collar on her coat. "I wish I'd ... *Mamma mia*, my mouth is already too frozen to talk."

Andri glanced at her lips, a way to warm them dashing through his mind. *Don't even think about it, Jóhannsson.* "The wind shifted so it's blowing straight over the Michigan peninsula from Superior. It'll change soon."

Gabby grunted. "And here I thought Chicago was a windy city."

He couldn't decide if she liked that fact, or missed the place she now called home. They fell silent as they neared town and he wondered if she felt the flood of childhood memories that hit him. Tabby had been born several years after he and Ruthie, so she had never tagged along with them on their adventures as they, with Gabby, had explored every inch of the island.

The town itself had not grown over the years, not that there was anywhere for it to grow. Main Street was still

Main Street, with wooden facades and wooden sidewalks. The dirt road had been paved with brick. A single white clapboard church stood sentry at one end of the three-block town center; next to it was the schoolhouse. City Hall was towards the center, and across from it stood the jailhouse.

Andri and Gabby passed by Jakobsen's Diner, which was closed, and Miss Lydia's Kitchen, which was open. The seamstress, the baker, the butcher—Kristiansen's Grocery where Tabby worked was closer to the schoolhouse—nothing much had changed since they were kids. Did Gabby appreciate the nostalgia or find the lack of progress off-putting? Andri couldn't read her neutral expression.

The cold had kept the street blessedly empty. In no time, he opened the jailhouse door for her and Freya.

"If it isn't Gabriella Salatino." Chief Michelsen's voice boomed around the open room that housed their desks. The large man rose from his chair and held open his arms. Gabriella walked into them without hesitation. "I've missed you, Salatino."

Gabby's giggle was muffled by Michelsen's girth.

The chief set her away from him, but kept meaty hands on her upper arms. "I hear you got yourself in a spot of trouble, too. Sit and tell me everything. Ah, but first ...

Jóhannsson, add a log to the stove and help the lady with her coat."

Andri made quick work of stoking the fire as Gabby settled in the chair across the chief's desk, Freya at her feet. The stove itself heated both the main room where Michelsen and Andri had their desks, but also the two cells located through the open hall behind the stove's potbelly. Empty, like usual. Andri pulled his desk chair around to sit beside Gabby.

Michelsen leaned back and scratched his blondish gray beard. "This morning, I met the officer who escorted you to the island. What was his name?"

"Wilson," Andri ground out, noting the pink darkening Gabby's cheeks. Freya raised her head at the irritation in his voice.

"Apparently he kept watch on your house, Jóhannsson." Michelsen watched Andri for his reaction, and anger morphed into embarrassment as Andri realized he hadn't noticed. Then again, neither had Freya. Where had the officer been that neither of them saw him?

"He took his assignment too far." Gabby waved her hand. "Did you speak with his superior? Detective Arthur. He's the man investigating my colleague's ... and my ..."

"The word *murder* is difficult to say, is it not?" Michelsen smiled at Gabby like a father would when doting on his child. "Brings back memories, I know."

Andri cut his gaze to Gabby as she nodded. Realization at what a thick-headed fool he'd been heated his insides. He knew she had just experienced the anniversary of her mother's death, which was still an unsolved murder. Why hadn't he at least acknowledged that? How could he be so caught up in seeing her again, in remembering what happened *after* her mother's death that he overlooked the obvious?

"Can you separate what happened then and what happened yesterday morning?" Michelsen continued, his focus where Andri's should be.

"Yes." Gabby gave a firm nod and pulled out her sketch pad. "I made sketches of the scene. Billy's room had been searched like mine. I couldn't discern that anything had been taken, certainly not from my room, so I have no suggestions on what the man had been looking for."

"You're certain it was a man?" Michelsen took the pad from her after she opened it to a specific page.

"No question, sir." Gabby's fingers wrestled in her lap and Freya rose to shove her snout beneath them. Gabby rubbed the dog's ears. "The man chased me from the house. He was not as tall as you and Andri, but big enough. I didn't recognize him."

Andri pressed his elbows on his knees. "You didn't

mention he chased you." She'd obviously gotten away, but what if she hadn't?

"Have you sketched him?" Michelsen turned the page in the notebook.

Gabby shook her head. "I'm not sure why, but I can't bring myself to ..."

Andri held himself still to keep from comforting her.

Michelsen glanced up at her with compassion. "Do not try, Gabriella. Hear me?"

"Why shouldn't she?" Andri asked, confused at the undercurrent between them. It didn't seem to be wholly about sketching the murderer, though Andri didn't like the idea of her drawing the man either.

"She is an artist who should be sketching beautiful things." Michelsen slapped the sketch pad on the desk, making Gabby jump and Andri flinch. "Not murderers and crimes and dead bodies."

Gabby raised her chin, her fingers deep in Freya's fur. "But I remember things, sir. I can help. You see the scene I sketched. Surely something can help us make a connection between why Billy is dead and I'm ... here."

"You're here to keep you safe." Michelsen glared at her. "Not investigate."

"All I ever do is draw wealthy people in pretty settings." Gabby raised Freya's nose to her own. "I want to do more."

The chief sighed, and Andri was grateful he and his boss were in agreement on that matter. The last thing Gabby should be doing was ... more, especially when it came to investigating murders.

"When Billy and I work together, he writes about the events I draw." Gabby stroked Freya's pointy ears and the dog relaxed under her ministrations. "We don't submit salacious gossip even though his editor would like us to. I draw pictures of events from galas that anyone else would see if they'd attended. It's not like either of us reveals secrets for an editor to publish."

The way Gabby carefully chose her words had breath building in Andri's lungs. She didn't submit the gossip, but that didn't mean she didn't draw it. She might not share secrets with Billy's editor, but who did she share them with? Because the elite always had something to hide, and Gabby all but admitted observing those things.

However, one look from Chief Mickelson had Andri holding back the question he wanted to ask. Instead, the chief spoke. "Perhaps your colleague chose to tell one of those salacious stories?"

Her fingers paused at the tips of Freya's ears, then continued rubbing the dog's fur. "How would the man even know we knew what we shouldn't know?"

With such convoluted wording, she was definitely hiding something. Andri leaned forward. "Gabby, why were you at your colleague's house on a Sunday morning?"

Her cheeks darkened. "Not for anything untoward."

"I wouldn't think so." But she had called Saturday night to escape a clingy gentleman. Was it Billy whom he'd had to scare off? Or someone else? "You seem to have attracted the attention of several ardent suitors."

"You know what, you're right." Gabby jumped to her feet so fast, Freya had to scramble out of her way or risk getting her paws stepped on. "This is all my fault."

Andri gaped at her. "I didn't say—"

"These men keep wanting to call on me." Gabby flung her arms into the air. "Is it because I am kind to them? I do not mean to encourage them. Still, they keep asking me no matter how many times I decline."

An uncomfortable feeling tightened his chest. Was she also talking about him? Or had he tripped over a clue? They'd been having a civil conversation and this reaction was more than his question warranted.

"Why do they all think I'm always interested in them?" Gabby leaned her palms on the back of her chair. "Why does everything have to be about romance? Or a relationship. My friend was murdered and my room searched."

How had he made such a mess of this? "Gabby …"

"I'm a professional artist." She snatched her sketch pad from Michelsen's desk and shoved it in her satchel. "I have a job to do and it is insulting for everyone to think otherwise."

"Gabriella." Chief Michelsen stilled her for a moment. "We said nothing of the kind. Sit down. This is an overreaction."

Her jaw dropped, then firmed. "I'm going to Ruthie's." She grabbed her coat and fled the building.

Andri and Freya jumped to follow, but Michelsen stopped them. "Let her go, son."

Andri still opened the door and commanded Freya to stay by Gabby. His dog tore after her at a sprint. He watched Gabby greet Freya without breaking stride, without glancing back to see whether Andri would join them.

While he was not a master at interviews, he'd sat in on many while working on the peninsula. The last few minutes revealed much. What it all meant, how it fit into her colleague's murder, or whether it had been personal … it would take time to tease out. Would she let him explain he hadn't meant to upset her? That he only wanted answers to keep her safe?

The cold air caused a shiver to arch through him, but he waited until Gabby turned the corner toward Ruthie's house, taking her out of sight. He stepped to the stove to add another log, letting the heat chase away the chill, then dropped back into his chair.

Michelsen raised his brows.

Andri crossed his arms. "She knows more than she said, sir."

"I'm aware." Michelsen drummed his fingers.

"And her dramatic reaction to my question? Obviously, a sore spot."

"Yes, I believe it is."

Andri barely resisted rolling his eyes. This wasn't like his boss. "We should talk about what she said, discuss the information, and determine a plan to keep her safe. She shouldn't be walking to my sister's house without a bodyguard."

Michelsen cocked his head. "When will you admit how you feel about her?"

"Sir?"

"It's obvious you carry a torch for her, Jóhannsson." Michelsen motioned toward the door Gabby had exited. "Does she know?"

His heart pounded and he stood, paced. He wanted to talk about Gabby, the case, not ... himself. "I'm not going to be like one of the men she just spouted about, if that's what you're worried about. I know I had my less-than-stellar days, but I have never mistreated a woman. I'm not going to act dishonorably toward her. You have my word."

"I didn't say you would."

"Good, because she needs us to focus on keeping her safe. She needs protection, and I won't risk that by kissing her."

Michelsen snorted. Then his laugh grew so that his large frame shook in his chair.

Andri glared at him. "It isn't funny, sir."

Michelsen only laughed harder, swiping at the tears squeezing from his eyes. Had the man lost it?

"She just went running, what's to say she won't keep going until she's off island?" Again. He'd made that mistake once already. "I ask a simple question and it's like I lit a firecracker. I don't understand why, and now you're laughing about it."

"Oh, son." Michelsen finally caught his breath. "I didn't say a word about kissing the girl. But obviously it has crossed your mind."

Andri froze. He repeated his words in his head and realized what he'd said. Mortifying heat made him wish to melt into the plank floor. His chin dropped to his chest, all indignation gone.

Michelsen chuckled. "I've known you care about her, but didn't realize it's more. This is good. You should find her, drop to a knee, then take her to the preacher. That way she won't need to worry about these other suitors and you can protect her without disrupting your mother's schedule."

"Sir!" Andri jammed his hands through his hair until they rested at the back of his neck. Why didn't the suggestion set off alarm bells? Only more self-consciousness?

"You can always ask her." Michelsen shrugged, as if he wasn't talking about *marriage*. Then tapped a stack of papers on his desk. "Her life is in danger, I have no doubts about that. These are the notes Officer Wilson delivered to me this morning. Detective Arthur kindly shared his investigation thus far. I don't believe Gabby realizes her colleague wasn't just murdered. He was beaten first."

"That's why nothing was taken." He needed to find her, convince her to stay by his side at all times. "It wasn't a theft. The murderer wanted information. Something Gabby must know."

"She might not know she knows." Michelsen tugged his beard. "I agree that she and Billy were investigating something. Secrets have a way of getting revealed, but it always costs."

Andri agreed. "Do you think she'll answer my questions if I try again?"

"You can try, but keep her close, Jóhannsson. If your feelings for her get in the way, deal with it. Is that understood?"

Before Andri could respond, the jailhouse door banged open and Joel Jakobsen stomped inside with an icy gust. "What is wrong with this town? Someone broke into my safe last night and stole my weekend earnings."

Michelsen stood. "Andri, get Freya. Joel, start at the beginning. What happened?"

Thirteen

Gabriella buried her face in her hands. "I made a mess of things."

"I'm sure you did not." Ruthie placed a steaming cup of tea on the table in front of Gabriella. Jack slapped two wood spoons together while leaning against Freya near the stove. "Now tell me exactly what it was that you made a mess out of."

Gabriella peeked through her fingers. "First, I got all defensive because of Andri's questions, then the chief told me I was overreacting. Worse, I knew I was, but that didn't stop me from storming out."

Ruthie laughed. "Being told we are overreacting usually causes a bigger reaction."

Gabriella sighed. She appreciated her friend's

understanding but … "It's highly embarrassing, Ruthie. Andri didn't deserve it."

Ruthie lowered herself into a chair, rubbing her large belly. "What did Andri ask you?"

Gabriella ran her finger along the rim of her mug. "About men who refuse to take no for an answer." Heat rose in her cheeks.

Ruthie's long fingers slid toward Gabriella, stopping just short of touching her wrist. "You know how protective he is of us girls."

Gabriella hid behind a sip.

"What aren't you telling me?"

Gabriella closed her eyes. "I think he took it personally."

A cold, canine nose pressed her side and she scratched Freya's ears.

"I think I reacted more to his reaction than his words. I don't think he's one of those men, Ruthie. He's nothing like …" Thomas Cook or even Billy. "How am I going to show my face to either of them again? They already think I am some … flapper."

"They do not." Ruthie's sharp reply brought Gabriella's attention to her friend. She had her arms crossed over her belly and the darkest scowl on her face. "If either of them took a minute to think about what you've been through, they would be a lot more compassionate."

Defensiveness rose. "They just want to keep me safe."

Ruthie sighed. "I know that means they had a single focus on the investigation, and not your feelings. They needed information from you, no matter how they had to get it. But it doesn't mean I have to like it. Andri is my brother, but you're my friend, and I don't like it when my friend gets hurt."

Gabriella tucked her chin to hide her smile. Freya's tail wagged, then she returned to Jack's side, letting the boy hug her neck.

"We got distracted." Ruth sipped her tea. "Continue. You were giving them information about the investigation?"

"I explained my sketches and why I think the person who killed Billy was looking for information. There has to be a connection there somewhere, between why Billy was killed and why my room was searched." Gabriella glanced at her friend. "I thought we were having a good conversation as we worked to figure out what connected those two things. And then Andri asked about all these men like I'm some loose woman or something, and it all exploded."

Ruthie's head tilted to the side. "Why did it bother you that Andri asked you about these other men?"

Gabriella straightened in her chair. "What do you

mean?"

"I'll rephrase: Why is that the question that upset you?"

Gabriella watched Freya and Jack as she considered the question. "It took away from the conversation. I do not like being treated like a girl instead of a colleague and a valuable part of the investigation. It felt like the only thing I have to offer is a pretty face, and I'm tired of nobody looking past my outward appearance."

"You can't deny the fact that you are pretty."

"I can and I will." Gabriella glared at Ruthie. Ali always admonished that quality of work had nothing to do with looks. "It has no bearing on whether I can do my job. As it is, I get dressed up for these galas, then all everybody looks at is how exotic I am with my dark skin, black hair, and brown eyes, rather than the reason I am there."

"Gabby."

"I can remember things and turn them into a picture with a pencil. Why does nobody think that is a significant skill that can actually help solve a crime?" Even Ali didn't want her investigating. "It's not just an excuse to share salacious gossip or secrets. My art can be used for justice, too."

The ticking of the mantle clock in the front room filled the silence. Jack banged the wooden spoon on the floor, his accompanying song a mismatch of words that sounded suspiciously like a Norwegian county rhyme Gabby remembered from childhood.

A log shifted in the stove and Ruthie rubbed her belly. "Who is it you want to find justice for?"

"Everyone. Anyone." Her foot tapped to Jack's *akka bakka* rhythm.

"Come now, Gabby." Ruthie chuckled. "I know you better than that. You have someone in mind."

Gabriella sagged, but kept silent.

"Perhaps the two men sitting in that police office don't think you can be useful or that your artistic skills are something that can help them, but why let it stop you?"

Gabriella studied her mug, letting her friend's words settle.

"When Andri suggested these other men only look at your pretty face, this is true, which is why you reacted. But what made you mad was when the chief ordered you to calm down. You didn't feel like you were being heard." Ruthie's voice dropped as Freya barked, causing Jack's chin to quiver.

Gabriella scooped him up and set him—with his accompanying spoon—on her lap so Ruthie wouldn't need to get up. Startling moment banished, he returned to *Akka bakka*, hitting the table in rhythm. Freya trotted to the door, tail wagging, which meant someone friendly had arrived. Aaron? Andri?

"Trust me, Gabby," Ruthie continued, quick and hushed, as if knowing their conversation would be ending soon. "When my husband says the same thing to me, I get just as mad. We've been married awhile and have had to learn to communicate better. Aaron is a natural leader, which makes him a very good mayor, but he fell in love with me because he can't boss me around."

Gabriella chuckled with the memory of the sparks that flew when Aaron had to work with Ruthie on a community dance. The man had been in awe of her the instant Ruthie systematically explained why his way of organizing wouldn't work. Completely smitten, Aaron begged her to help him and not only had she been right, her ideas had made the event spectacular. The two had married months later and now Ruthie managed her household with the authority of a general while offering her husband her ideas to make the town a better place.

The back door opened and Andri entered with a greeting to Freya before holding up a hand to keep Ruthie from rising. He shot a glance at Gabriella before returning his attention to Ruthie. "I need Freya. We have to get to work."

Jack scrambled from Gabriella's lap and raised his arms for Andri to lift him. With a grin, his uncle swung him in the air, the action doing something odd to Gabriella's middle.

"Did something happen?" Ruthie's worried question snuffed the joviality from the room.

"Nothing dangerous." Andri shifted his feet as he again swung a giggling Jack in the air again, belying the gravity of his explanation. "But Gabby, would you join me? I don't like bringing you to the scene of a crime, but for your safety …"

And the safety of Ruthie and her family. Gabriella rose. "You're right, of course."

She shrugged on her coat to avoid the siblings' silent conversation. Ruthie would never acquiesce so quickly, and the fact she hadn't said a word of protest worried Gabriella. And Andri? She'd never seen him so awkward, except after she surprised him with that kiss. Gabriella's body heated. Maybe returning to Heima Island hadn't been the smartest decision.

Ruthie touched Gabriella's shoulder, making her jump, and pulled her into an awkward hug, her large belly between them, and whispered, "I do not think your disquiet has anything to do with Andri or the chief. You want to feel useful and you want to use your art for a reason, so when men you respect did not offer that to you, it hurt."

Gabriella swallowed against the truth. While gently delivered by a loving friend, it stung.

"Gabby, we need to go," Andri said from across the room.

Ruthie squeezed her tight, her unborn baby kicking against the pressure, and again kept her voice low. "I wonder, Gabby, if illustrating galas is enough for you."

Gabriella touched her friend's stomach, feeling the baby move again. Ruth could always read her mind, like Ali, which is probably the real reason her boss sent her to Heima Island. She knew, like Chief Michelsen, that Gabriella would want to investigate, which meant shipping her out of the city so she couldn't follow through with it.

Yet, this was why she and Billy had been digging into questionable practices among the elite. It was also why she'd never given up the investigation into her mother's murder. Her art could solve ... Gabriella groaned.

Ruth clutched Gabriella's shoulders. "You figured it out."

Gabriella nodded, feeling foolish, especially with Andri watching the exchange. It had nothing to do with him ... well, mostly ... and everything to do with Ali and the chief. And now she needed to apologize for overreacting, just as Chief Michelsen said.

Andri handed Jack to his mother, the little boy clutching the spoon to his chest with one hand, other thumb in his mouth as he rested his blonde head on her shoulder. Almost naptime, Gabby suspected. As Andri stepped back, he glanced at Gabriella. Ruth watched the interaction between them as she adjusted her son on her hip. Gabriella knew she needed to apologize, and it appeared like Andri wanted to say something. Gabriella's stomach twisted.

"I'm sorry." The words croaked from her throat. "You asked a legitimate question back at the station and I got mad. I was unprofessional. I'm sorry."

Andri's shoulders dropped, not in relief, but defeat. "You don't need to be professional with me, Gabby. I'm your friend. Friends can get angry at one another. I asked a question I probably should not have. I also hadn't meant it to be a personal one. I want to keep you safe."

Ruthie grinned. "Look at you two talking like adults. This is wonderful. Now I need to get to my chores and you have a crime scene to investigate. Andri, you keep Gabby in your sights. Do not let her run away again, am I clear? And Gabby, you stay by Andri no matter how infuriating he gets. I don't care what protest is forming in that mind of yours. It is for your safety and I am putting my foot down. I do not need to be worrying about either of you. This baby is causing me to lose enough sleep. I do not need to lose any more."

"Yes, Mother." Andri grinned at Gabriella, who grinned back.

"I saw that!" Ruthie rolled her eyes. "Now off with you both."

Fourteen

Andri rolled his shoulders and inhaled. The sun had warmed the air though the wind blew briskly. He found it invigorating. Or maybe that was due to breaking through the tension between him and Gabby.

He glanced down at her. She and Freya were carrying on a conversation about Jack. Gabby might be doing all the talking, but he knew his dog well enough to see understanding in Freya's intelligent eyes.

You want to feel useful and you want to use your art for a reason, so when men you respect did not offer that to you, it hurt. Ruthie thought she'd been whispering, but Andri had caught her words. It'd been the smack upside his head he needed. Their friendship ran deep. An awkward kiss shouldn't have destroyed it, and he knew a way to begin rebuilding it.

Andri cleared his throat as they turned into Main Street. "As I said, I don't like the idea of bringing you to a crime scene, but I agree with Ruthie that you need to stay close."

Gabby rested her palm on Freya's head. "What was the crime?"

"Oh, Gabby." He gently stopped her with a hand to her arm. How could he have been so calloused? Of course she'd be worried about going to a crime scene. Her home was one. "It was just a theft at Joel Jakobsen's diner. Nothing grisly."

She chewed her lip, weighing his words.

He shifted. Should he share the idea Ruthie's whispered comment had inspired? "I thought ... Your sketches ... Maybe you ..." He was butchering this olive branch.

Her head tilted, wonder lighting her brown eyes. "You want me to help you investigate?"

Andri nodded, the rightness of it settling in his chest. "It's not only an opportunity for you to stay where I can keep you safe. You have a talent, Gabby, and I'd be foolish not to ask for your help."

Gabriella's smile bloomed, smacking into him like a wave. "You won't regret this, Andri. It's the least I can do for you."

He grunted to cover unwelcome emotions. "Let's go.

Jakobsen is angry enough without us making him wait longer."

They crossed the street to where Jakobsen paced in front of his family's diner. While Andri had never considered his former schoolmate's looks, he couldn't help doing so now since Gabby walked at his side. Would she prefer a beanpole over a boulder? Not that Jakobsen was skinny, exactly, but Andri was large in every way. Not fat, just ... big. And Gabby was not.

Or perhaps she would like brown hair instead of fair, like that cop who escorted her here. Even Jakobsen edged toward a darker blond than Andri's hair. Jakobsen was also a successful business owner, not a policeman. Andri barely held in a growl. Why did it matter to him when men of all kinds flung themselves at Gabby? As would be illustrated in *three ... two ... one*.

"Why, if it isn't Gabriella Salatino." Jakobsen turned from his pacing with a grin. "I heard you were back in town, but I wouldn't believe it until I saw you with my own two eyes."

"Hi, Joel." Gabby smiled back. Did she also step closer to Andri? He glanced down to see her gloved fingers entwining with Freya's fur. Huh.

"What are you doing with this lout?" Jakobsen jabbed his thumb at Andri.

"She is assisting in the investigation." Andri yanked his notepad out of his coat pocket. "Did Chief Michelsen already discuss what happened?"

Jakobsen scowled. "Lydia called him over to her place. Apparently, the crime scene at my place of business isn't as important as whatever she needs."

Andri struggled to keep his face neutral as irritation spiked through him. The chief knew what he was about, but that was unprofessional, and Andri was sure Lydia hid something. Did the chief know what it was? Was he protecting Lydia for some reason? Andri shook his head. He trusted the chief, but he didn't like the doubt that clung to the back of his mind.

"I guess I'm stuck with you." Jakobsen shoved his hands into his coat pockets. "Let's go inside. I'll show you what happened. Can I make you a coffee, Gabriella?"

"Oh, sure." Gabby's voice at his side yanked Andri back to his previous thoughts. She never agreed so easily with him. They always ... bickered, fought, found ways to poke at one another. Now, she followed Jakobsen inside, leaving Freya standing in the door, her expression asking whether Andri planned to join them.

Andri entered the dim interior of the diner. Where Lydia's Kitchen had light walls and checkered tablecloths, Jakobsen's had dark walls and worn tables. Jakobsen held a chair at one of these and Gabby sat, then pulled out her drawing pad. Freya joined her for a moment, then returned to Andri's side. Time to get to work.

"What time did you notice the money missing?" Andri asked Jakobsen.

"First thing." Jakobsen waved him toward the wood counter. "Since food service doesn't begin until the lunch rush, I don't arrive as early as Lydia. As soon as I walk in, I stoke the stove fire, then empty the safe and take the previous day's deposit to the bank."

Andri followed him past the till, then through a pair of swinging doors into the kitchen. A long table took up most of the space and behind it was a massive wood stove. Jakobsen turned right and headed to a closed door beside a large ice box.

"This is my office and there's the safe. It was open and empty when I arrived." Jakobsen crossed his arms as he stood out of the way as Andri approached the small door in the wall with the combination wheel in the center. "I know it's not state-of-the-art, but I've never had someone crack it before."

"Who knows the combination?" Andri peered inside. Not a coin had been left behind.

"No one but me. And before you ask, what reason would I have to steal from myself?"

Andri chuckled. "That was my next question. Your answer?"

Jakobsen's shoulders dropped. "That money is what I need to buy the food I prepare. It pays the lumberman I get wood from. It pays the couple waitresses who help out on busy nights. If I pocketed the money, how would I keep my business? And if I wanted to give it up, what's stopping me from selling or simply leaving?"

"You've given this some thought." Andri leaned his hip against Jakobsen's desk.

"Not much else to do once your boss left this morning."

"So, someone stole money from Lydia's till, then—"

"She deposits her money at the end of the day, so there's nothing in her till in the morning except on weekends." Jakobsen held up a hand. "I know this because she scoffed when I had this safe installed."

Andri whistled for Freya. "Shall I see what Freya finds?" Or would Jakobsen obstruct his investigation like Lydia had?

"Have at it. I don't have anything but food in my cellar." He rolled his eyes, then shrugged. "I'll get Gabriella coffee. Will you have a cup?"

Taken aback by the kindness in the offer, Andri hesitated a moment before he nodded. "Thanks, Joel. I'll have it after I see what Freya finds."

EYEWITNESS SKETCH

Andri watched the man leave after giving a whispered greeting to Freya as she trotted inside the room, too many thoughts jumping around his head to settle on one. "Let's get to work, girl."

Fifteen

Gabriella sat at the table where the men had left her and sharpened her pencil with the little pen knife she kept in her satchel, then set to work. Slowly, the diner around her appeared on the blank page. She'd sketched rooms like it before. The dark walls, large counter, brass till ... it reminded her of a speakeasy.

She turned the page of her notebook and sketched the image that came to mind. Men with glasses filled with amber liquid. Women with long necklaces and feathers in their hair. While she couldn't draw the sound of jazz music playing, she drew a couple dancing in the middle of the room. Then she shaded the image with a haze of cigar smoke.

It had been a long time since she'd been in one of those

places. Carrie and Lena would follow a story there, but Ali insisted Gabriella stick to galas and balls where wealthy men did similar activities as in a speakeasy, but behind ornate doors with enough money to keep the police away.

Gabriella assessed her drawing, the picture reminding her of the first time she visited a speakeasy. Billy had gone with her. It had been her first assignment with him and it had been an awful experience with handsy men in a room too dark to draw. However, it had formed her friendship with Billy and proved his character to Ali, especially when he had to step in as her protector. Could they have seen something on that trip that came back to haunt them now? It had been years, so it didn't seem plausible.

But perhaps it was as probable as anything.

Beside her, Freya's ears perked at Andri's whistle, and she trotted away. Gabriella returned to the present scene, switching to a fresh page. This time, she sat back and sketched her impressions. What would this room look like if it were filled with people? In a dry town such as Heima Island, customers would not be men drinking alcohol, but families enjoying a meal together. Though, how did a family afford such an expense these days? Perhaps one of the fathers was behind the theft in a misguided effort to feed his family.

Just as she flipped to a new page, Joel emerged with a

steaming cup of coffee. She let him settle it on the table so she could avoid their fingers accidentally touching. She knew he would want to flirt with her. And without Andri here as a buffer, tension built in her shoulders.

She forced a smile. "Thank you, Mr. Jakobsen."

"We're old classmates, so it's Joel." He offered that grin she remembered from their youth and sat at her table. "How have you been? It's been a while since you've been seen in town. A decade almost? How have you been keeping yourself? No ring on that finger."

She covered her left hand with her right. Perhaps if she wore a ring, she could pretend she was engaged? Maybe that would be better than calling Andri to play her pretend beau. "I work as an illustrative journalist. Andri asked me to sketch the crime scene here."

"Then what are you doing sitting out here? Shouldn't you be in the back sketching my safe?" Joel leaned back in his chair, obviously not intending to escort her there.

"I will when Andri is ready. Right now, I am sketching this area. Have you seen business grow or lessen in the last year or so?"

"Since the crash you mean?" Joel was a smart one. She remembered that about him from their school days.

Looks and smarts were not always a great combination. She had noticed that it frequently led to pridefulness and overconfidence, which she usually found extremely intimidating. Yet, as Joel sat comfortably in his chair at her table, she didn't feel that way with him and it freed her to turn her concentration toward the puzzle. Her pencil began sketching and, in a moment, Joel appeared on her page just as he looked in his chair right now.

"I would say business has been the same, if a little less." Joel spoke as if a full minute or three hadn't passed. "Most people around here are unaffected by what happens in the nation itself. We aren't a big city dependent on factory work. We are fishermen and lumberjacks and shop owners. This is our quiet time of year anyway, with the shipping lanes closed down for the winter. Though there are plenty of men who desire a warm meal and don't have a wife to cook it for him."

Gabriella took a sip of coffee, the bitter brew warming her. "Do you like being the one to cook for them?"

The expression of surprise that lit his face said he'd never considered that before. "Plenty of men cook in restaurants and diners. My father owned this, and my grandfather before him, back when the ships were much more plentiful. My mother and grandmother never helped out here and as an only child, it fell to me."

"And no wife to help you?" She probably shouldn't ask such an impertinent question, but he had already pointed out her ringless finger.

Joel shook his head, a somberness to the way it moved. Then he peeked at her and grinned. "Interested in filling the position?"

A laugh jumped out though no words came with it.

"Something sounds funny." Of course, Andri chose that moment to appear.

Embarrassment heated Gabriella's face and she was grateful for her darker skin that hopefully hid the blush that was sure to be darkening her cheeks.

Joel stood. "Just entertaining the lady until you return. I'll get your coffee if you want to show her the safe so she can sketch it."

Andri's jaw dropped and neither he nor Gabriella managed a word before Joel disappeared into the kitchen. Joel was not the youth she remembered nor the man she expected, and it seemed this wasn't his usual behavior either because Andri was as surprised as she.

"Are you still interested in sketching the safe?" Andri rested his hand on the back of her chair.

Gabriella nodded and switched to a fresh sheet as she followed him behind the counter, through the kitchen where Joel had a cup of coffee waiting for Andri. She should have brought her own cup along.

Andri showed her the location and went back to get his

coffee. The quiet rumbling of the men faded as she took in the back room and sketched it. Then she approached the safe, drawing first the outside and then the inside. Something would jump out at her eventually, but for now she just soaked in the space and let the images sear itself into her mind before she returned to the men in the kitchen.

She could sense something was off about the room, but she couldn't pinpoint it, so she committed it to paper and memory. Perhaps in the morning, when she drew her impressions, she would figure out what seemed wrong.

SIXTEEN

ANDRI PAID FOR SANDWICHES from Joel's diner and carried his and Gabby's back to the jailhouse. Joel had wanted to offer them as a thank you for investigating the theft, but Andri didn't want it to look like a payoff.

Gabby's tension increased the closer they came to his office and he realized the last time she was there, just a couple hours ago, she had stormed off after he had made a mess of things.

He elbowed her shoulder. "I'm sorry again for this morning. You were right to get frustrated with me. You have a talent that we would be unwise to ignore."

"That wasn't the full reason why I was upset." Her steps slowed and he matched her pace. "And actually I wasn't all that mad at you. Kind of."

"I'm glad to hear that. I can't help feeling protective of you, you know. You can always tell me I'm being a bear. How else am I going to learn unless I have someone pointing out my flaws? Like my sister reminding me I could learn some humility."

"There are always people who will point out your flaws." She kept her gaze on her feet as they closed the distance to the door of the jailhouse. "Do you have people who will tell you what you do well?"

The thought struck him upside the head. Did he? More importantly, did she?

Gabby opened the door before he could get it for her. Chief Michelson glanced up from his desk and Andri knew he needed to talk to his boss again as well. He needed to understand why the man was protecting Miss Lydia. It had continued to niggle at him since he had first wondered at it again this morning, and he needed answers.

He opened his mouth to offer a greeting when he realized that Gabby had gone straight to sitting behind Andri's desk without saying hello to the chief. Andri looked between them and the chief raised his brows. What had Gabby said? That Andri wasn't the only reason she stormed out of here earlier? Andri replayed the conversation in his head and realized he wasn't the only one who had made a donkey of himself.

"Say what's going on in your head." Mickelson directed the order at Gabby.

She glanced at Andri then back at the chief and shook her head.

"Gabriella. Speak."

Andri barely managed to keep his feet planted. He wanted to put himself between Gabby and his boss's fire.

"Would you like to see the sketches I made of the burglary at Joel's?" Gabriella sat at Andri's desk and opened her satchel.

Obviously she wasn't going to explain, but Andri didn't think it was his place either. He rested a hand on Freya's head, unsure what to do.

"I see you brought lunch." The chief pointed at the sack in Andri's free hand. "Did you bring one for me?"

Why hadn't he thought of that? He was distracted by a pretty woman, that's why. "I'm sorry, sir. I didn't even think. I'll go back." After setting the bag on his desk, he glanced at Gabriella to confirm this was all right. At her small nod, he turned to go. As the door snicked closed, Freya at his side, he heard Gabby speak.

"I'm not investigating like you think I am." She fired the words so they came through the door easily. "It's never far from my mind and if I ever have information, I will give it to you. So stop treating me like the little girl who lost her mother. I am fully capable of managing my own affairs."

Andri backed away, deciding not to interrupt. His boss did not need him witnessing such a dressing down. Though, the picture raised Gabby even higher in his esteem. He was proud of her for standing up for herself and admired that, while she might criticize his boss, she refused to do so in front of his employee, in front of another man.

As he waited for his order, Andri let his mind run through their cases. He and the chief hadn't been able to discuss the delivery of the barrels from the other night. Did that have anything to do with the break-ins at Lydia's Kitchen or Joel's Diner? He would need to ask the chief about why Lydia wouldn't let them fully investigate ... Or perhaps she simply didn't want Andri and Freya to investigate.

Joel wrapped up Chief Michelson's sandwich and handed it to Andri with a nod, and Freya followed him back outside.

Gabby told the chief she wasn't investigating her colleague's murder, but Andri suspected she wanted to. Why had she agreed to being protected here? Had she even been given the option? He didn't know enough about the case, and that wouldn't keep her safe.

She was right that whomever ransacked her apartment could easily track her down. He needed more information, and from now on, he'd make sure that he or Freya was with Gabby at all times. He glanced at his dog as he let her into the jailhouse. She didn't like to be away from him, but hopefully, she would accept Gabby enough to guard her.

Tension still radiated from the two within the building, and it kept conversations stilted and unhelpful. The three of them did what they could as they danced around awkward questions. They analyzed Gabby's pictures, considered the information that Officer Wilson left with the chief about Holland's murder, and tossed out possibilities for who might want to steal from the two food places in town.

As the sun began to set, indicating the end of the work day, Gabby held up a finger, stopping the conversation. "I've been thinking about this since I sketched Joel's diner. A father in a tight situation wouldn't want to steal food – he wouldn't want to risk his wife asking where it came from. However, if he stole money, knowing he would return it by buying food from the very places he stole from, then the food itself would be free and no one else would know about the crime."

"Insightful." Andri sorted through the papers on the chief's desk to find the sketch she mentioned. "I hate to accuse a father with a family in need."

The chief huffed. "Theft is still against the law. Motive has no bearing. The injured parties need recompense, and that's why we are here."

Something inside Andri wanted to argue that point. Justice must be served, but the thought of hungry children twisted his stomach.

"I think that's enough for today." Michelsen stood. "Get home before dark and, Andri, keep the lady safe."

Gabby's cheeks darkened and she buried her face in Freya's fur.

This far north, even as the daylight hours grew longer, they had yet to reach the point where there was equal daylight and darkness. And here on the island, with nothing but water surrounding them, night was dark indeed.

The following day, Andri left Gabby and Freya at the jailhouse while he asked around about any suspicious behavior. Between the two thefts, the smugglers, and any outsiders who might be looking to harm Gabby, it wasn't difficult to ask general questions. However, no one had seen anything out of the ordinary.

Wednesday, Chief Michelsen spent his morning at Lydia's Kitchen and once Joel's diner opened, Andri and Gabby spent the day there. Andri didn't mind Joel attempting to flirt with Gabby. Since Monday, she'd grown quieter, rarely offering the smile Andri enjoyed seeing so much. Even Joel couldn't bring a genuine light to her eyes.

With no movement on any of the cases, including no news from Detective Arthur on the death of Billy Holland, Thursday brought about a rather ordinary day. Andri hoped it would help Gabby's spirits, but one glance over her shoulder as she worked on her morning sketches proved him wrong. For the first time since she arrived on Heimi Island, her drawing paper was blank.

Andri exchanged a worried glance with his mother. She's been uncomplaining about spending the night here, however she'd arrived later and later each night since the Berg children had come down with something. Andri hated the suspicion that Mr. Berg could be behind the thefts. Searching for work on the peninsula gave him an easy alibi, however, it wouldn't be difficult to return overnight, and he had at least once Ma said.

"Are you feeling alright, Gabriella?" Mom pressed her wrist against Gabby's forehead.

"Of course." Gabby's false cheer slipped under Andri's skin like a sliver. "Sometimes it takes my muse a bit to wake up in the morning."

Whether Mom accepted that as truth or not, she

shrugged. Andri, however, kept a close eye on Gabby throughout the day. She seemed a shell of herself and not one drawing appeared as far as he could see. Instead, she seemed to stare at that white page as if it were a mountain to conquer or a battle to wage.

Even the chief seemed to notice her behavior, and he shared concerned glances with Andri every so often as they talked over the cases. They had nothing to go on, no new information, no new leads or even suspicious activity they could act on.

Nothing.

SEVENTEEN

About mid-afternoon, Chief Michelsen slapped his hands on his desk. Freya barked once, indignant, and Gabby's mouth quirked to the closest semblance of a smile he'd seen in days.

"We are getting nowhere." Chief leaned his palms on his desk. "We can't find the barrels. The thief seems to have vanished. And Detective Arthur called me today to say all his leads have dried up, too."

"Have you spoken to my boss, Ali?" Gabby asked, hope flitting across her face.

The chief shook his head and Gabby's shoulders fell.

She shifted the papers she had laid out on Andri's desk. "I'll send her a telegraph when we're done here for the day."

"Andri, take her to the post office now, then call it a day." Michelsen crossed his arms. "We need a change of pace. Maybe it will inspire a new perspective."

Andri had seen it happen before. As much as he wanted to solve the cases, he mostly prayed the early evening would give Gabby whatever she needed to break through her slump. Perhaps he could help. They didn't need to go directly to the cabin. Spring had attempted to show her head today, so perhaps they could take the long way back to his place.

With silent understanding, Andri and Gabby donned their coats and headed for the post office, which also held the telegraph office.

"Do you know what you want to ask your boss?" It was a silly question, but Andri needed to fill the silence between them.

"Ali has a code to follow. For the girls who go undercover, it's more elaborate. For me, I usually telegraph the solicitor's office that works as a go-between. But now, because of what happened to Billy, she set up a different system for me."

"So you cannot contact her directly?" It sounded like espionage or police work, not journalism.

Gabby rested her hand on Freya's head. "I told you, Ali is also Mrs. Griffith Moorland. That echelon of society doesn't know she's also Ali Di Stasio. Nor do they know her *nom de plume*. She and Carrie are very careful about keeping those identities separate to protect themselves."

"Don't take this the wrong way," he said, hesitating outside the telegraph office, "but it doesn't seem safe."

"For a woman?" Gabby raised her brow at him.

He rubbed his neck. "Yeah."

"I don't think it's safe for a man or woman, but it is necessary." Gabby scratched behind Freya's ear. "There is a lot of corruption, and there are a lot of shady practices, all hidden by powerful people. I see it when I attend these galas and am grateful for journalists like Ali and Carrie and Lena who shine a light on it."

"Do you want to do that kind of work?" *Please say no.* He wasn't sure he could stand by if she put herself in danger.

Fortunately she shook her head. "I want to do more than draw pictures of wealthy people at galas, but I don't know how my colleagues handle the different identities they have to manage. It's hard enough being me."

If they hadn't been standing on Main Street, Andri would have pulled her into a hug. Instead he pulled open the post office door. "I'm glad you're you, Gabby."

Telegram sent, they began the walk back to his cabin. Somehow, this felt more intimate than simply walking to and from work. Perhaps it was the warmer weather or the slower pace or the fact he was leading them the long way back to his place?

His neck heated as he remembered the chief's suggestion to offer Gabby a marriage of convenience. Making a life-time commitment to make a few days easier made little sense to him, though, no matter his feelings for Gabby. The Chief seemed to know more than he said, and Andri didn't like it.

"Could we detour by the lighthouse?" Gabby's question pulled him from his thoughts.

The pain-filled wistfulness in her eyes stopped him from denying her request. "Sure, Gabby. C'mon." He took her hand, not willing to let her face these memories alone.

They walked along the craggy north side of the island, a red sunset building behind them, leafless trees hiding them from the rest of town. Across the choppy water, cast in pinks and purples, the coastline of Washington Island stood about three miles away. Seagulls cawed overhead and Freya trotted beside them.

Andri adjusted his grip on Gabby's hand. "I'm sorry we haven't found the person who killed your mom." He'd been investigating since Gabriella had left the island, though only since he'd become a Heima Island officer did he have access to the official file. It was disturbingly thin.

"There wasn't much to go on." Gabby's voice was already quiet, yet it was softer still as she added, "Not officially anyway."

Should he ask what she meant? No. He could later. Right now, he needed to be her friend, not a cop. "Do you miss the island?"

She nodded. "But I've found a place to belong in Chicago. Ali, my boss, is Italian like me, and the building she owns, where I live, is at the edge of an Italian neighborhood. It makes me feel close to the memory of my parents."

"I wish I could see it." The words slipped out before he had control of them. Yet he wasn't sorry. He did wish he could see Gabby in her element. He missed that.

"I wish you could meet Ali." Gabby chuckled. "She's smaller than me, but makes up for it with a vibrant personality."

They came to a rocky edge and Andri climbed down, then helped Gabby safely descend. Freya had no trouble bounding after them.

"She became an orphan in the Chicago Fire and grew up at the orphanage behind St. Mark's—that's the church across the street from the Di Stasio building. Along the way she met a wealthy businessman and married him, but continued working as an independent journalist. Over the decades, other female journalists have come and gone within her agency, but she's remained the heart of it."

"I'm so glad you found her."

"Are you?" Gabby stopped them around the bend from the lighthouse where they'd first met all those years ago. "Are you glad I left Heima Island and became a journalist?"

He turned and realized they stood inches apart. The sunset created a golden halo around her dark hair. Unable to resist, he lifted his free hand to her cheek. "I am glad you found a home, but I'd be a fool not to admit I wished that home were here."

Her bottom lip disappeared between her teeth. Freya leaned against his leg.

Did he risk fixing his mistake from seven years ago? He eased closer, drawing their clasped hands to her hip. Her brown eyes searched his face, looking for what, he didn't know. He only hoped she could see how much he cared about her.

His chin dropped. She knew he cared, but thought of him like a brother. If he crossed this line, if he kissed her, he needed to be sure about his feelings for her. *Caring* wasn't enough.

The chief's suggestion of marriage again came to mind. Andri hadn't balked at it, only been embarrassed that his emotions had been so clear. But Gabby had made a new home. If he wanted to be in her life as more than a friend, then he'd need to follow her there. That meant leaving Heima Island, his family, his job, the house he'd built.

"Andri?" Trepidation wrapped around his name.

His heart fissured and he knew. He'd give up everything to see her happy. "I love you, Gabriella Salatino."

Shock registered in her eyes and he ducked to give her the kiss he should have given her all those years ago. She didn't respond at first, but neither did she resist, so he released her hand and wrapped his arm around her back, pulling her to his chest. This time, she kissed him back.

Eighteen

Andri was kissing her. She was kissing Andri. In the fading light of sunset as waves crashed against the rocks on which they stood. Her fingers longed for a pencil to draw the scene, to capture the wonder that filled her heart.

Then Andri slid his hand from her cheek to her neck and she was lost. This wasn't the tentative kiss of their youth that she had given him. Andri kissed her like a man who knew exactly what he wanted. Her. And unlike the other men who thought her a loose woman, an easy mark, a girl willing to give more than she wished, Andri's hold was protective, sheltering.

He broke their kiss with a heavy sigh and rested his forehead against hers. "I've wanted to kiss you since the day you kissed me, but I needed to grow up and get taken down a peg. I see that now."

Gabriella eased away just enough to see his eyes and read his expression. She understood what he meant, but didn't know what to do with the information or the feelings that swirled inside.

He traced her jaw with his thumb. "I'm going to keep you safe." The way he said it sounded almost desperate, like he'd do anything ...

She shook her head. "No. I know you, Andri. You cannot put yourself in harm's way. I can't—" *lose you*. But a sob kept her from saying it.

Thankfully he didn't give her a pat on the head and tell her he'd be okay. No one knew that for sure. Just ask her mother. She'd been in the wrong place at the wrong time and paid with her life. Andri, however, would choose to put himself in danger if it meant protecting her.

"Stop thinking, Gabby." Andri slid his arms around her in a tight hold, her cheek pressed against his chest, his large frame shielding her. "I know it feels like we can't solve this, but we will. Or in some way make sure you're safe without being stuck here."

A smothered laugh slipped out. "I am a bit stuck."

She wiggled and Freya stuck her lean body between them. Andri released her with a grin, then held out his hand. "Let's go see the lighthouse then get back to the house. Dark falls quickly once it sets its mind to it."

The easy companionship they'd had as youths settled between them now. For the first time since she witnessed her mother's murder, she felt as if she could expand her chest to take in a full breath. At the turn before they reached her old lighthouse home, she tugged Andri to a halt and closed her eyes. She tightened her grip on his hand and let the freshwater scent of the lake and bay fill her senses. With it came the memories.

Ruthie dragging Gabriella on an adventure, Andri gamely following. Warm summer nights. Frosty winter days. School lessons and community picnics. A childhood uninterrupted by the death of her father because her friends refused to allow her to fade into the sorrow. They faced it with her, shared stories of before, and insisted on new memories after. Until ...

Tears stung her nose. "I'm sorry I kissed you that day. I'm sorry I destroyed our friendship. I-I missed you."

"Oh, Gabby." Andri pulled her to himself again, his cheek on her head. "You didn't destroy our friendship. If anyone did, it was me. I shouldn't have let you run. But I was a foolish kid who didn't know what love meant."

"It wasn't just the kiss." The realization hit at his mention of *love*. Whether the love of a sibling, a friend, or something more, how could any type of love be love when secrets wedged between them?

Gabriella pulled herself away from Andri's hold. Sure, she'd been embarrassed when he hadn't kissed her, but that wouldn't have destroyed the depth of their friendship. Not if that had been the only thing between them.

And it stood between them now, that eyewitness sketch.

She spun and hastened toward the lighthouse, Freya on her heels. No, she ran from Andri. She was repeating the past, just as she promised herself she wouldn't do. Seven years older and what had she learned?

The lighthouse keeper's cottage was a squat, square structure beside the white tower of the lighthouse that rose up on the edge of a cliff. The beam sliced through the gathering, warning ships of the danger at Death's Door, though not that many ships passed this way anymore. They took the safer path by Sturgeon Bay.

"I'm not letting you run this time." Andri's voice in her ear made her jump. She turned to find his jaw set in that way she knew meant business. "I'll follow you to Chicago if I must. I didn't kiss you for the fun of it, Gabby. You mean too much to me for whatever this is between us to be a game. It's not something I take lightly or treat as a fun pastime. You are worth more than that, especially to me."

The more Andri talked, the harder Gabriella's heart

pounded. She backed away, words catching in her throat. He couldn't talk like this when she held this secret. It'd been eating away at her for days already. All she could see when she stared at her blank page was the face of her mother's murderer. Yet she couldn't will her pencil to draw him again. Not since that first sketch she gave to Chief Michelsen seven years ago.

Suddenly, Andri grabbed Gabriella's forearms and yanked her. She screamed as she tripped over a rock and landed on the ground, Andri stumbling beside her. Freya's snout tucked under her chin, forcing her to lay on her back. Cold soaked in and she shivered.

"Are you alright?" Andri leaned over her, breathing hard. "You nearly tumbled off that cliff. It's like you disappeared on me and all I could do was grab you."

"Everything okay out here?" A male voice called from the lighthouse.

"Just fine. Trying to keep the lady safe," Andri called back, then helped Gabby to her feet whether she was ready to stand or not. Freya stayed close.

"She alright?" asked the lighthouse keeper. At least, she assumed it was him seeing that he stood by the lighthouse.

"Are you?" Andri assessed her.

She nodded, though she wasn't sure of the truth of her reply.

"Bring her in. My wife has coffee on the stove." The lighthouse keeper waved them closer.

Gabby wasn't ready to go inside. Not now. Not yet.

"My ma is meeting us at my place." Andri must have sensed her tension.

"Even better." The man still watched from his place by the lighthouse.

Andri tucked her against his side. "I've got you, Gabby. We'll talk once we're at my house."

A shudder quivered through her. Only Chief Michelsen knew she could identify her mother's murderer. And Ali had somehow figured it out. If she told Andri, what would he do with the information? Would he demand she sketch the murderer's likeness as he'd suggested about Billy's murderer? Would he wonder why she had kept this quiet all these years? Or question why it had been left out of the official report? Would he think less of her for being unable to help solve her mother's murder these past seven years?

Her fingers drifted to her lips. The kiss she had longed for, had convinced herself she would never experience, had been more wonderful than she had imagined. Yet, with this secret between them, she couldn't allow another. Even their renewed friendship had a crack in its foundation until she revealed the knowledge she kept hidden away.

"You're thinking again, Gabby," his voice rumbled. "We

might have been separated by seven years, but it cannot undo the friendship of our youth. I know the way that little V settles between your brows ... you're working through something. Won't you trust me with it? Once we're safely back at my house?"

"I want to." The admission echoed in her soul, strengthening her resolve. "I'm scared, Andri."

Freya must have sensed her trepidation because she tried to maneuver between her and Andri, but Andri kept his leg close to hers, forcing Freya to walk on Gabriella's other side.

"Perhaps once we are inside." Hope and wistfulness accompanied his words. If she didn't tell him, she sensed he'd be disappointed. Not because he wanted to know her secret, but because he wanted her to trust him.

All the times she'd turned to him for help over the past years, he'd never let her down. Annoyed her, sure. But she could trust him. Never had she doubted that. What she needed wasn't trust, it was courage to finally loosen her tongue and share what she'd witnessed with the man she trusted most.

Silence wrapped around them like the night air. Gabriella was grateful to be left to wrestle her own thoughts. As they turned down the drive that led to Andri's house, he stumbled to a stop. The fading sunlight barely shown through the trees, but it proved just enough to reveal fresh tracks in the muddy snow. They led toward his front door, and did not lead away again.

"Has your mother already arrived?" Even as Gabriella voiced the question, the tensed set of Andri's shoulders told her the answer.

Freya sniffed at the prints, rapidly following them to the cabin. Andri's palm went to the pistol he'd been keeping on his belt and he edged himself in front of Gabby. She rested her hand on his shoulder blade. Together they followed Freya to the house.

NINETEEN

Andri tensed as Freya sniffed her way up his porch steps. His grip tightened on the butt of his pistol, and he ignored the feel of Gabby's hand on his back.

Freya nosed the door and gave her tail a wag. Breath rushed out of Andri's lungs. Whomever had let themselves into his house was likely family, not a stranger, and definitely not dangerous.

Gabby stayed close as he pushed open his front door. Freya bounded inside, but Andri's greeting died on his lips.

"What are you doing here?" The accusation jumped out of his mouth before he knew what he was saying.

Tabby crossed her arms. She stood in the middle of his kitchen, her hip jutted out. "Hello to you too, Brother."

He hadn't seen his sister for over a week, and something seemed different about her. He narrowed his gaze, assessing. Same blonde bob hairstyle his father forbade. Same long-sleeve pink flowered dress he remembered her wearing to the winter dance a few weeks ago, because she made him twirl her so it swung around her knees. Same pale features that ran in the family.

"Finished giving me the cop stare?" She rolled her eyes in true Tabby fashion.

Andri huffed and would have said something big brother-like except Gabby rested her hand on his forearm, disrupting his brain's electrical circuit.

Tabby gave Freya's sides a rub. "Mom had to stay at the house tonight because the Bergs needed her help. Mrs. Berg is sick now and Mr. Berg hasn't been back in two nights."

His sister kept her focus on Freya as she talked, but Andri didn't miss her swallow. She might try to appear indifferent, but something about the situation bothered her.

With a slight shake of her head and a pat to Freya's shoulder, Tabby straightened with a false smile. "So Mom insisted I bring you dinner." She cut a glance at Gabby, who stood quietly at his side, having closed the door and now was letting the siblings work things out amongst themselves, just as she'd done in their youth. "It took you long enough to get home, brother dearest, but perhaps I understand why. Which means it's time for me to leave."

"You can't." Again the words jumped out of his mouth, firm, and without the gentle coaxing his headstrong baby sister would need if he wanted her to listen to him.

Tabby raised a white brow. "And why not?"

He forced a deep breath to make sure his tone changed. "Do you remember Gabriella Salatino? She's staying here for a few days and Mom has been our chaperone. If she isn't here, that responsibility falls to you."

"Chaperone? Really, brother? You are a full adult and a policeman. And I didn't bring a change of clothes. I have no night dress and no dress for working at Kristofsen's tomorrow."

He ignored the first part of her statement for the landmine it was. "I'll run home and get clothes for you." He'd leave Freya. Surely if he was quick about it, Gabby would be safe.

Tabby rolled her eyes. "You won't know what to get me and I don't want you touching my unmentionables."

His neck heated. She had a point. "But you can't go outside in the dark alone. It's not safe."

Tabby flopped her arms, drawing Freya to her side. "It's Heima Island, Andri! I will be fine. I walked over here alone and I can walk back. You have been a cop too long, seeing shadows where there aren't any. There are no criminals on this religious rock of an island. Gracious, people probably don't even know Gabby is staying here, your house is so far away from everyone else's. I can go to sleep in my own bed, where it's comfortable."

Tabby's speech had wound him tighter and tighter so that his teeth clenched together to keep from spouting unhelpful words. "You'll take my bed, just like Mom. And I won't let you walk outside in the dark alone. It is not as safe here as you think it is, Tabby. Yes, I'm a policeman. I know things I don't share with you. Can you please trust me on that?"

The look in Tabby's eyes said she was mounting another defense, which he knew would push him past his ability to keep his tone civil. Fortunately Gabby, the angel that she was, intervened.

"Must you two fight?" She stepped between them, a palm raised to each. "Andri, your sister is an adult and capable of making responsible decisions without a big brother's critique. And Tabby, please understand our situation. Yes, we are adults, but we need a third party here to keep the gossips from spinning tales. Plus, your brother is right, it isn't safe for you to walk home at night right now."

Tabby's brows crashed together at the phrase *right now*. "Why not?"

The hint of something vulnerable in his baby sister washed his anger away. "Because someone wants to hurt Gabby and I'm afraid that person could find her here. It's my job to protect her. I need your help, Tabby."

She glanced at Gabby as if for confirmation, then nodded. "Alright. I'll stay. But after supper, I need to get my clothes."

Andri knew better than to argue that point.

"Then let's eat." Gabby shrugged out of her winter coat, then helped Tabby get their meal onto the table while Andri gave Freya her supper.

Usually he waited to feed her until after he ate, but he didn't want to give Gabby an opportunity to slip out. After supper, he'd leave before Tabby could. Not that he wanted to leave Gabby alone, but he could leave Freya with the girls while he ran to their family's house.

Then he could ask his mother to pack Tabby a bag and ask why she hadn't insisted Tabby bring a change of clothes along in the first place. Perhaps it had been difficult enough to get Tabby to bring food over here and Mom hadn't had time to fight her on the details. Anyway, her staying with them tonight would be an opportunity to talk to Tabby about whatever it was she'd been into lately that had their mom so worried. The *religious rock* comment concerned him because he'd once felt the same.

He said grace for their food, but the silence hovered as they ate. Andri should probably prompt conversation, since this was his house, but his thoughts gripped him.

Yes, between whatever Tabby had gotten into, the smuggling, the thefts, the danger to Gabby, there was no way he would let Tabby or Gabby go outside alone in the dark. And the more he considered the danger to the two women seated at his table, the more strongly he knew he needed answers. The food sat in his belly like a rock and he set aside his half-empty bowl of soup. He didn't look at either woman as he pushed away from the table.

"Andri." Tabby's tone was dubiously suspicious. Tough.

Instead of replying, Andri instructed Freya to guard, grabbed his coat, and was out the door before he'd even put it on. The cold air snaked around him and he quickly donned his jacket and shoved his hat on his head.

"Andri!" Tabby shouted after him, but he had already rounded the corner and jogged away before she could think of following him.

As he hastened to his childhood home, his thoughts tumbled with his next steps. Chief Michelson's suggestion that he marry Gabby shoved its way to the top, swirling with memory of their kiss. The chief was right that it would solve the problem of needing a chaperone, but he wouldn't force Gabby into that untenable position unless she chose it. Chose him. And something held her back. Whatever she feared was stronger than her trust in him. Could he convince her that she had nothing to fear from him?

He hadn't let the words *I love you* escape without thought. He did love her. More than he realized when he told her, more than he realized before he kissed her. Before today, he'd thought he simply missed his friend, regretted letting his youthful pride come between them. But now he understood she had always held a piece of his heart.

The crunch of old snow behind him had Andri spinning around, his hand going to the pistol he now kept at his waist. Except a fist landed squarely in his jaw.

Before he could get his brain unscrambled, the attacker grabbed him by the shirt.

"Leave it alone." The man's lips moved beneath the fabric of his mask. Then he shoved Andri to the ground and leveled a kick to his temple before Andri could protect himself.

"Leave what?" Andri blinked to refocus his eyes as he tried to keep up with what his attacker was saying and where the next blow would land. He pushed to his feet unsteadily. His large body felt more like a rock, weighing him down.

His attacker aimed another right hook. Andri blocked the blow, but it knocked him off balance and he was too heavy to keep his feet under him. Nausea churned the little food in his stomach as his legs buckled.

"Stop investigating." With a grunt, the attacker stomped on the side of Andri's knee, bending it at an unnatural angle. Andri cried out as pain shot fire from his knee.

The man took off and Andri rolled on the ground a bit, fighting the blackness from his dizzy, pounding head and the agony in his knee. He had to get help. Not for himself. The girls, Gabby ... they were alone and his attacker could go after her next.

TWENTY

"WHY WON'T HE EVER listen?" Tabby huffed as she sank back into her chair at Andri's table. Freya followed, plopping down at their feet with an echoing grunt.

Gabriella smiled. "He's a protector, Tabby. You should know that about him by now, considering he is your brother."

Tabby scowled, then her expression turned speculative. "Is what he said true? That you're here because someone tried to hurt you?"

Gabriella hesitated. How much should she share with Tabby? Aunt Deb had confided her worry over her youngest child and based on the attitude Tabby had given Andri tonight, Gabriella could understand why. Yet, having spent the last few years under Ali's guidance and living with independent women like Carrie, Lena, and Emma, she saw Tabby's behavior a bit differently.

She slid her bowl out of the way and leaned her elbows on the table. "Yes, I'm here because I witnessed a murder and my room was searched."

Tabby's blue eyes widened, and her mouth slipped open.

"I know being around me may not be the safest choice, but I do appreciate it." Gabriella reached out an open hand. "If you would stay, it would be a relief to me. I don't want Andri to feel as if he was compromising."

"Wait." Tabby cocked her head. "Isn't it *your* reputation that he's worried about? Not his? It makes no sense. Mom, Ruth, and Andri always tell me that I need to be worried about how people view me, that my reputation is all I have, and that if I'm ruined, it will ruin my life."

This time Gabriella had to cover her mouth to keep her lips from quirking. Tabby had a bit of Emma in her. Always wishing to push boundaries of what females can do. Emma considered sports her personal megaphone to show that women can be just as strong, and fast, and amazing as men.

Tabby folded her arms, obviously preparing to deliver a triumphant ending. "And I don't see how it's anyone's business what I do with myself. Nor do I understand why people's opinions have anything to do with who I am or what I can do."

Yup. Emma Hancock when she first arrived at the Di Stasio building a couple of years ago. Gabriella remembered the twinkle in Ali's eye well. Could she guide Tabby similarly to how Ali had mentored Emma, at least for the short time she was here? She could certainly try.

Without a word, Gabriella pulled out her sketchpad and pencil. Freya lifted her head from her paws to watch her, then returned to her nap. With quick strokes, Gabriella swiftly drew the outline of a cabin window, making it the focal point on the page. Tabby watched with a skeptical expression that grew more and more curious as Gabriella drew a man who looked like Andri. She faced his back toward the window, then drew a woman who looked like her facing him, her side in profile.

"What is it you want me to see?" Tabby studied the image.

"There isn't anything I *want* you to see." Gabriella continued to shade the image. "I want you to see what you see."

"I see a man and a woman talking to one another. They're inside, but there is nothing bad happening between them. Why would I assume that there would be more going on?"

This time Gabriella let herself smile. The young woman's innocence was refreshing after the years of illustrating the wealthy at their galas. "I'm glad you asked and I'm equally happy nothing untoward filled your mind. Now, allow me to add color."

Freya ignored her as Gabriella withdrew her colored pencils. She used them rarely as they were one of her most prized possessions and she wanted to make them last as long as possible. However, for this situation, it seemed a necessary use of them. She didn't waste the lead on the exterior of the cabin. Instead she created a soft glow of light inside the window. Then she shaded Andri's blonde hair and the tan shirt that he wore today. Finally, she moved on to herself, giving the woman in the picture the same clothes she now wore.

She turned the picture to Tabby. "What do you see?"

"I see the two of you. Again, I see nothing bad going on. You are simply standing there in a room talking. At least, I assume it is you. It is your clothes, but why have you not colored her face and her hair?"

Without a word, Gabriella turned to a new page. This time, she sketched the cabin window again but turned the man so he faced outside and the woman with her back to the viewer. She used her colored pencils to draw Andri, as in the first picture, then she darkened the woman's hair to an ebony and her skin to a bronze. She sketched the woman so that her chin dipped in a demure, feminine way, then turned the picture back to Tabby.

"Well, this girl doesn't appear to be you." Tabby tapped the woman. "She's not wearing your clothes. It's another woman. I know Andri doesn't have a girl and she doesn't look like she's from around here. Everybody on the island has blonde hair. Except you."

Tabby blinked as if she saw Gabriella for the first time. Gabriella nodded for her to keep talking.

"I never really noticed that you don't look like the rest of us because you were always Andri and Ruthie's friend. You were like a big sister. Always around. Until you weren't. I didn't really think about why or notice that you were ... different."

"Keep thinking out loud," Gabriella encouraged.

"So, when I thought the picture was of you, I knew you and Andri were friends. Nothing would happen that would require a chaperone any more than it would if I stayed here, or Ruthie."

Not quite, but Gabriella kept the memory of Andri's kiss to herself.

"However, in this second picture, I didn't recognize the woman ..." Tabby's words trailed off and her cheeks pinked.

"And you assumed Andri had a girl you didn't know about."

Tabby nodded. "Why did I think that? I know it's not true."

"I am often asked how I can call myself a journalist when I simply draw pictures. But I drew two similar pictures, yet each told an opposing story. With the power of this sketch, I managed to put doubt in your mind about your brother's integrity. Why would he have a woman you didn't know in his house? We assign meaning to images based on our own experiences. You know me, but I haven't been on Heima Island in seven years except to briefly visit Ruthie. How many residents would remember me, especially when no one is supposed to know I'm staying with Andri?"

"It wouldn't be your reputation at stake." Understanding lit Tabby's eyes. "But Andri is a policeman, the pastor's son, an upstanding member of the island. If his reputation takes a hit ..."

"There's more to it." She turned back to the first picture and filled in the woman's face, dipping her chin in the same way she drew the second woman, darkening her hair and skin in a similar way. Then she showed it to Tabby. "Is this first woman the same as the second?"

Tabby took the sketch book and turned between the

two pictures. "Other than the clothing, yes they do seem like the same person. But the first one I know is you. The second I assumed I didn't know because she looked different, and flirty, and—ohh."

"This is why he is so insistent that you stay here with us tonight. You know me, your family knows me, they would not worry about what could be happening here because they know Andri would protect me like he would you or Ruthie. But others don't know me. Andri himself has commented on how many men ask me to dinner. Like you said, I stand out in this town because I look different. I am memorable when I walk down the street. If they see me with Andri, they will make the same assumption you did."

"But it's not true, nor is it fair." Tabby crossed her arms. "Your reputation matters, too."

Gabriella swallowed back the emotion clogging her throat. "Andri agrees with you."

"Why did you leave?"

"I left because my mother had just died and I was young and alone and confused and needed to find my wings. I suspect very much that you and I are not all that different, and that if you lost your mother right now, you might make similar choices as I did." Gabriella caught herself before she slipped up and mentioned the youthful kiss.

"Speaking of my leaving, it does not take him this long

to get home and back. Do you think Ma succeeded in waylaying him? She's been skeptical about my activities lately."

"And what activities do you think your mother is so worried about?" Gabriela flipped to the second page. "Do you suppose she worries about a picture such as this?"

"I wish I had a beau." Tabby blushed but shook her head. "Honestly, I'm putting in extra hours at Kristiansen's. Everyone expects me to act a certain way, follow all the rules, and it makes me feel like a chain is wrapped around my chest, especially being the pastor's daughter. At least when I'm working at the grocers, I feel like a grown woman. Mind you, I don't want to do something bad or foolish, but everyone assumes that, because I am not the good little girl they think I should be, I'm doing something wrong."

"Then perhaps staying here with your brother is just the opportunity you need to be on your own for a little bit. Andri can keep an eye on you, which will make everybody happy, but then you and I can get to know one another as well. What do you think?" Another idea slipped into Gabriella's thoughts, one Andri would likely hate.

Tabby tapped on the drawing pad. "We can help one another. I'll make sure people know that you are a good woman and that Andri is keeping you safe. Nothing untoward happening here. And I do want to hear all about being an illustrator journalist. Did you know I read *Illinois Life* every week looking for one of your drawings? Ruthie has a subscription and I always make sure to read her copy."

Gabriella smiled, then glanced at Andri's mantle clock. "It is taking him a long time." Much more time had passed than she thought.

Tabby took their bowls to the washbasin. "Should we call Mom?"

Gabriella looked down at Freya who raised her beautiful brown gaze to hers. Now that Gabriella wasn't focused on Tabby, worry crept in like a rapidly rising tide. "You finish the dishes. I'll make that call."

And when Aunt Deb answered, she sounded surprised that Andri would be expected there. He had never arrived.

Twenty-One

"We're going to find him." Gabriella grabbed her winter coat, her brusque actions bringing Freya to attention.

"I hate to be the voice of reason." Tabby dripped water as she hurried over without drying her hands. "But if someone wants to hurt you, Andri disappearing could be a way to get at you."

"Exactly." Gabriella shoved on her hat. "I'll take Freya. She'll find Andri and keep me safe enough."

Tabby grabbed her arm, causing Freya to nose between them. "Andri was worried about my safety just walking home in the dark. I get the feeling he would like it even less if you went out there."

"I know." Gabriella buttoned her coat. It might be

March, but here on the island, spring came late and the cold held on without the sun to warm the lake-washed air.

"Gabby!"

"What? I'm going. You stay here in case he returns. Or your mother calls."

"I think I'm seeing even more clearly," Tabby muttered. "You care about my brother, and I suspect he doesn't see you like a little sister, like me. That picture you drew, the second one? That was the true picture. You're his girl."

She couldn't deny the possibility, seeing as how he told her he loved her and kissed her the way he had.

Tabby sighed. "I might get annoyed at Andri for his big brother protectiveness, but he protects those he loves. And if he loves you, and you get hurt, you'll break his heart. Maybe protectiveness runs in the family because I can't let you do that."

This time Gabriella grabbed Tabby's arms, earning a rumble from Freya. "I can't sit here knowing the danger I brought to the island could be the reason he's in trouble. Is he hurt and can't get help? Did my attacker kidnap him or—" Her voice broke.

"Fine. Give me a spare sheet of your drawing paper. We'll leave Andri a note in case he returns while we're gone." Tabby speared her with a glare. "Don't balk. I'm going with you."

Gabriella probably should've begged Tabby to stay safe at home. If she got hurt because of Gabriella ... but right now, gratefulness to not have to search for Andri alone was all she could manage. "Thank you, Tabby."

"I've always thought of you as a big sister, like Ruthie. Maybe you'll be one for real some day."

Gabriella's face heated, but secretly, she thought the same. While Tabby dressed, Gabriella left Andri a note. "Should we call Aunt Deb?"

Tabby shook her head. "I've discovered that when it comes to my mother, sometimes it's better to act first. That way when all is well, she can't argue in the first place."

Gabriella rolled her eyes, but gathered the lantern and stepped outside. "You know that's why she worries about you, right?"

"I'd just like to not be treated like a little kid."

"I don't see you as one right now. But Tabby, if there's danger, you have to run for help. Please."

"Should we tell the chief?" Tabby closed the door behind her.

Gabriella shook her head. Whenever she'd needed help, she'd always turned to Andri, never Chief Michelsen. That fact now gave her pause. "I suppose, like with your mother, I don't want to waste time arguing. Let's go. Freya, find Andri."

She and Tabby had to jog to keep up with the dog's quick pace. They circled around the back of the house, the lantern showing footprints clearly in the muddy, leftover snow. Finding Andri should be easy, but what if someone else lay in wait?

This section of the island was covered in rocks and tall grasses. No one had built in the area, leaving it natural and wild. To the left, the ground rose to the rocky cliff where the lighthouse stood sentry.

Right and straight ahead, the grassland would give way to the flat area where the town had developed. The Jóhannssons lived in the parsonage house next to the white church on the opposite side of the island.

So much ground to cover. Perhaps they should have called for help. Yet, the island wasn't all that large.

Tension gripped the back of Gabriella's neck, tightening more when Freya turned, not toward town, but toward the lighthouse.

"Why did he go this way?" Tabby breathed hard as she kept up.

Gabriella wished she knew. The lighthouse stood out like a welcome signal. A sign of home, one full of happy memories. She loved the old structure, but if Andri had sought help there, the lighthouse keeper couldn't leave his post. Not at night, not unless a seafaring danger required his aid. Like the last time she'd seen her father.

Tension morphed into nauseous fear. Had Andri walked this way of his own accord, or had he been taken this way? Her pace quickened despite the stitch in her side. Freya must have sensed her emotion because the dog ran faster.

"I ... can't ... keep up," Tabby huffed. Gabriella slowed, but Tabby waved her on. "I'm going to town for help. If he went this way, we need a search team."

Gabriella swallowed. Nodded. Tabby meant search boats. Because the only thing beyond the lighthouse was the cold water of Lake Michigan.

Freya barked, Tabby gave a wave, and Gabriella tugged up her skirt to run faster. Freya dashed ahead. Without having to keep an eye on Tabby, Gabriella began to notice signs of someone having walked this way.

"Freya, wait." Gabriella dropped to a crouch. The ground had sketched a picture. She pulled out the small notebook and bit of pencil she kept within the inner pocket of her coat. Ali encouraged each of them to always carry pen and paper, no matter the type of journalist. Freya whined and paced, but Gabriella ignored the dog, quickly sketching what lay before her.

Here where the grass gave way to the craggy rocks that led to the lighthouse, the mud created a canvas she duplicated onto her page. Footsteps leading toward town with light indentation. Footsteps leading back to the water sat deeper in the mud and farther apart.

Comings and goings wouldn't have seemed odd, even ones that made it seem as if someone ran to the lighthouse. What had caught her attention were the drag marks. Someone had hauled something toward the lighthouse. It must be heavy because the pattern told of a lunge forward, then a pause.

A chill shuddered through her. If someone dragged Andri's ... body ... to the cliff edge, wouldn't the dragging be consistent? Or was that hope talking? She shifted to the side, looking for the footprints of someone who pulled a heavy object. As she'd illustrated for Tabby a mere hour ago, an image told a story, but that story could be interpreted in different ways.

"I'm not seeing another set of prints, Freya." Did that disprove her fear? Yes and no. If no one pulled a heavy object, that meant the object pulled itself. Following that logic, Andri could be alive, but injured. Then why didn't he pull himself toward town where a doctor could treat him? Why go uphill to the lighthouse?

She tucked the notepad and pencil back into her pocket. There were only two reasons Andri would drag his injured self away from help. Either someone forced him or he chose this way to protect ... her?

"C'mon, Freya. We need to find him." She'd made herself a promise that she wouldn't put him in danger. If the man who murdered Billy had found her here, she needed to make sure Andri wouldn't be the next dead body she found. She'd barely held herself together after losing their childhood friendship. She doubted she'd survive if she lost him now that she knew he loved her.

TWENTY-TWO

ANDRI RESTED HIS HEAD on the rock as pain washed over him. He'd managed to follow his attacker past the lighthouse and around to the rockiest part of the island shoreline, the part buffeted by the waves of the lake herself.

While the town and the ferry port were on the Green Bay side, this section was unprotected from the most dangerous part of Death's Door. Why had his attacker gone this way?

He forced his head up and blinked to clear the haze from his eyes. His knee had swollen so much that it stretched the seam of his trousers. Perhaps he should have hauled himself to town. He'd been lying in the grass, attempting to goad himself into moving, when his attacker—who else would it have been—ran past, heading toward the water.

If Andri could identify the man, he could put an end to …

Well, what he saw made no sense. Why was his attacker helping a female out of the fishing boat below and not at the regular ferry dock? Why attempt to disembark on the most dangerous stretch of island shoreline?

What he wouldn't give for a pair of binoculars or one of those pocket cameras he'd seen a tourist use back on the peninsula. Although, it was dark and, except for the lighthouse beam above and the lantern from the boat, he wouldn't be able to see at all. Lake Michigan was a black hole of slapping water.

Stars pocked the inky sky above. If Gabriella were here, and there was no danger, and he wasn't in pain … if all the good things aligned and he sat here with her, it would be a romantic moment, surely.

The boat's motor hummed louder.

Andri squinted in hopes of catching the name of the boat before it sped away. The man who had assisted the lady onto shore spoke to the captain, then offered a parting wave. Was the lady about to scale the rocks? His sisters and Gabby would have done it as youths, perhaps Gabby would do it still, but this woman? She wore a long straight skirt from what he could see of her silhouette, a fur coat, and a jaunty little hat. How was her escort going to get her up the craggy cliff?

He recognized neither of them—the distance could be why—but the more he studied the man as he lifted the woman into his arms, he realized this was unlikely to be his attacker. This man had a leaner build. The man who attacked him appeared more muscle-bound. Though this man certainly didn't lack in strength: being able to carry a woman up those rocks was no easy feat.

He'd wait here in the shadows until they'd gone, then he'd force his body to the lighthouse. The pain wouldn't be kept at bay for much longer.

He could commit their likeness to memory if only Gabriella were here. Had coming here been the right choice? He thought he'd been following his attacker. What if by detouring here instead of going to town for help, or even returning to his cabin, he'd left the girls open to attack?

The thought kick-started his heart. He couldn't wait for these people to make it up the rocks. He needed to go straight home. He tucked this good leg under his body, but the movement shot shards of pain through his injured limb.

Rustling neared as a cry threatened to scrape up his throat and he covered his mouth with the inside of his elbow. The others couldn't know he was here. Panic clawed at him. He couldn't allow them to get away if they were up to something nefarious.

And then a cold nose pressed into his neck. Freya. A wave of relief was quickly followed by fear. "How'd you get here, girl?" The words were barely audible, but he searched his dog's face in the intermittent beam of the lighthouse. No blood, so she hadn't fought off an intruder. How had she ...

"Andri." Gabriella dropped beside them, a lantern in hand.

He doused the flame, hoping the couple below hadn't seen it.

"Andri?" Gabriella lowered her voice to a whisper.

He put a finger to his lips, then reached for her hand. Gabriella was here. "Are you unhurt?"

"Yes, but are you?"

Gabriella was okay. She was here, with Freya, looking for him. Desperation gave way to overwhelming pain. He had to warn her about the couple, then he'd just lie here for a moment.

"There's someone—"

He squeezed her hand to silence her. She scooted closer, her free hand resting on Freya's collar, and her attention on the couple. They'd just reached the top of the cliff and the woman's unhappy tone floated toward them.

Gabriella leaned forward. "I know them."

Andri's gut twisted. He waited for her to explain. She seemed to think the same because she simply kept watching the couple. Andri closed his eyes, letting his body succumb its need for rest though he kept his ears alert. Freya would warn them if someone were coming, then he could react. For now, he needed to conserve his strength to keep Gabriella safe.

"They're gone." Gabriella spoke, albeit softly, after a period of time Andri couldn't account for. "Let's look at your knee. Did you fall?"

Andri shook his head.

Gabriella's cool fingers touched his jaw. "I didn't think so. This looks like a bruise from a punch."

"Ask your questions, Gabby." He didn't have the energy for the way she skirted the obvious. Freya watched them closely, likely reacting to the tone of his voice. He patted her head to let her know to stand down.

Gabriella pursed her lips. "We can't stay here. Let's go up to the lighthouse. Tabby went for help. We thought ... we thought you went into the water."

Like a splash from the cold lake, realization struck him. He struggled to sit up. "You thought I was dead?" Why hadn't he gone straight home? He could have alleviated her worry. Instead she was out here and in danger.

"Your path led toward the lake." She shrugged, but the

lighthouse beam flashed overhead, reflecting the glint of tears in her eyes. "Can you stand? Your path said you dragged yourself here."

"Wait." He captured her hand before she could rise. Freya's gaze bounced between them.

"A doctor needs to see to your knee." Gabriella's voice quivered, drawing Freya to her side.

"I'm sorry, Gabby." He scrubbed his face, wincing when his fingers rubbed his bruised jaw too harshly. "I let my pride get in the way of your best interests. I thought I could find my attacker. Figured he was the same one who killed your friend."

Her fingers wrapped into Freya's fur. "Was your attacker the man helping the woman up those rocks?"

He'd forgotten she said she knew them. "No. My attacker had thicker shoulders. Like mine. The man here was leaner. Who is he?"

"Not the murderer. I would have recognized him."

"Gabby. Who is he?"

"The reason I needed a pretend beau the other day. Thomas Cook. That was him. And I'm fairly confident the woman was Molly Zander."

"That doesn't mean anything to me. Why would they be here? If Cook came alone, I could understand it, but why bring a woman with him?"

"It means nothing good, I'm sure. But we can talk more once you have your knee assessed. You must be in great pain."

"Not moving helps." He tried to smile, but her concern didn't lessen. "You being here helps."

The corners of her mouth tipped up. He couldn't force himself to look away. Would a kiss give him the fortitude he needed to get to the lighthouse?

She covered her mouth. "Andri?"

"I'm sorry." He'd made her uncomfortable. "I can't think straight."

Quick as a hummingbird, she pressed a kiss to his cheek, then set his arm over her shoulders. "On three. Ready?"

No, but focusing on the feel of her lips on his cheek was indeed the edge he needed to get to the safe haven of the lighthouse.

Twenty-Three

As Gabriella waited to be patched through to Ali, she let the memories of the lighthouse keeper's home dance through her mind.

The phone box was on the kitchen wall, and like a moving picture, she could see her parents dancing together while her mother tried to keep supper from burning.

She could hear her father's voice singing in Italian as he readied to go out into a storm to check the lighthouse flame.

She could feel the lake breeze as she, Ruthie, and Andri raced home after school to be greeted by the scent of freshly baked bread.

"*La mia stellina?*" Ali's voice came through the earpiece and Gabriella shifted to speak into the cone mounted to the wall box.

"I'm here." She couldn't shake the memories and leaned her forehead on the cone.

The doctor who now treated Andri in the parlor was the same who'd declared her father dead. Not that there had been any doubt once his body washed up the morning after the storm.

Like the whiff of smoke came the memory of the sulfur from the gun fired by the man who killed her mother. Then came a blast from the shot that killed Billy. She could see the drag marks of Andri pulling himself to the cliffside a few hours ago.

"Sweet one," Ali's voice dragged her from the memories. "I'm sending Emma. I wish I could be there myself, but there are other matters I must oversee here. She'll arrive around midday. Or sooner if she pushes Griff's auto as hard as she'd like."

Gabriella chuckled as she knew Ali had hoped she would. "Emma does enjoy the speed."

"She's bringing news I won't share now. What else do you need her to deliver?" This was Ali's way of returning their conversation to the reason Gabriella had contacted her.

"Thomas Cook and Molly Zander are here on the island."

"You can confirm this?"

"I saw them."

"And you know it's them."

Gabriella huffed. She knew her boss held high journalistic ethics and made sure her journalists followed those rules, but sometimes she just wanted her eyewitness statement to be enough. However, like she showed Tabby earlier that evening, a picture without context could be misconstrued.

"I don't doubt you saw them." Ali's voice softened with compassion. "Under oath, would you have any doubt it was them?"

Ali would press until Gabriella explained. She sighed. "It was dark, Ali, but they had a lantern and the lighthouse beacon shone bright. Thomas Cook has a face I easily recognize, because it was just days ago that he put that mug of his too close to mine."

"Rather defensive, Gabriella." Ali didn't approve. Another of her ethics was objective reporting. It was Gabriella's too, but it was hard sometimes. So though she pushed against Ali's questions, in the end, she appreciated them.

Gabriella tempered her tone, sticking to the facts. "Cook has a distinct face I've seen enough times in a variety of lighting to recognize. Molly was recognizable because she appeared so out of place. She has distinct mannerisms and she exhibited those while she and Cook interacted. So, to answer your question, yes, I know it was Cook, but as for Molly, I couldn't swear under oath."

"Better." Ali's smile came through the line. "I'll have Carrie speak with Detective Arthur, Griff can see about Cook, and I'll see what I can find out about Molly. We'll send as much information with Emma as we can."

"Thanks, Ali." Tension seeped out of Gabriella. How she appreciated her boss and colleagues. "I miss you all."

"How are ... other things?"

Gabriella's cheeks heated, knowing full well what Ali was asking. "We ... he ... well."

"He finally kissed you, huh?"

Why did her boss have to be so direct at times? "I'm not sure what it will mean. And he was injured."

"What happened?"

"Someone attacked him and severely compromised his knee. The doctor is with him now."

"Go stay by his side. Emma will be there soon."

Gabriella nodded. "Thank you."

"Be careful, *la mia stellina*."

Gabriella agreed, even though she knew her boss meant more than her physical safety. Her heart was already at risk if something happened to Andri. And when everyone deemed it safe for her to return to Chicago? Then what?

She was saved from answering the question by the arrival of Andri's parents, followed by Chief Michelsen and Tabby. Gabriella tucked herself into a corner as they turned the interior of the little building into a whirlwind.

"You're Salatino's daughter?" The lighthouse keeper, a handsome man with short brown hair, came to stand beside her. His presence was solid as the activity swirled toward where Andri rested.

She nodded. The keeper and his wife had welcomed them without question, sharing food while they waited for help. Where the woman seemed as energetic as Ali, albeit several decades younger, her husband seemed a quiet, old soul, and she relaxed in his presence.

"I thought so." He gave her an empathetic smile. "You look like him. Did you know there's a plaque in the lighthouse?"

She'd forgotten about that. The town had sponsored it the year after her father drowned in his life-saving mission. Andri had a similar spirit, saving those who needed help. But sometimes heroes die.

"You look like you need air, and I need to check on the light." He inclined his head towards the door. "I'll let you in so you can see it."

Gabriella followed him and his lantern outside, the cool

air refreshing after the arrival of Andri's family. She knew they meant well. They loved Andri, but it hurt a little that no one checked whether she was alright. Selfish of her, sure, but no one had thanked her for getting Andri to safety or even acknowledged her presence.

The light above spun overhead, shining into the night. It went dark as the panels hid the beam from shining out over the town, then it appeared again as it shined out over the water. In Chicago, she often found herself by the harbor, watching the lighthouse beam call boats to safety.

"I'm sorry, I didn't get your name." She remembered her manners as he held the lighthouse door for her. They'd been so occupied with helping Andri, she never thought to ask.

"Collins." He shrugged. "I used to be part of the Coast Guard stationed at a lighthouse near Racine, but when my widowed sister died and left me with her children, I couldn't stay. I retired and the department sent me here."

"I'm sorry for your loss." Such an innocuous thing to say. "I can't imagine ..."

His eyes turned glassy in the lantern light. An odd sight in one so stalwart. "Loss is hard, especially when it is unexpected."

She could relate to that.

He turned for the stairs. "They talk about bringing

electricity to the island. It has its conveniences, but sometimes I like this old way."

Gabriella trailed her hand along the outer stone wall of the lighthouse as they wound their way up. How many times had she followed her father up these stairs?

"There he is." The lighthouse keeper palmed the plaque with her father's name. "You don't have to wait for me. Stay as long or short as you like."

"Thank you, Mr. Collins."

She nodded, throat too clogged to reply. The man was right. She traced her father's name. Papa had sacrificed his life for a stranger whose boat had capsized, only to be caught in the undercurrent as he tried to get the man to safety. She knew, however, that her father would do it again. He had spoken often of his job as a calling.

"My work is a calling, too, Papa. It might be dangerous, but how can I turn my back when people like Mamma and Billy need someone to find their killers? It's time to face the memories."

It was time to end this before someone else died. She'd leave Andri in his family's care and return to his house alone. She knew he'd send someone, or make his family bring him home, when he realized she was no longer at the lighthouse. While she waited, she would draw. She had two eyewitness sketches to complete before Emma arrived tomorrow.

Twenty-Four

"Thank you for staying." Andri accepted the cup of coffee from Tabby the following morning.

He lay on his bed, his leg cushioned and supported by a mound of pillows and blankets. It ached something fierce, but each time Tabby tucked snow-packed bundles around his knee he felt relief.

"How is she?" Andri glanced around his sister, not that he could see Gabby from here.

As far as he knew, she hadn't left the kitchen table since his family had delivered him to his house in the wee hours this morning. Nor had Freya left her side.

Thankfully, he'd convinced his parents and Ruthie that he needed to be here to heal properly

"She slept some after you arrived." Tabby lowered her

voice. "She was mighty worried about you last night. What are you going to do?"

"What do you mean?"

Her cheeks pinked. "You two obviously like one another, but she lives in Chicago and you live here. Even I know married couples don't live that far apart if they can help it. And surely not newlyweds."

"You're too smart for your age, Tabs." Andri covered his own embarrassment with the tease. It also bought him time to think of a way to dodge the question to which he had no answer.

Tabby crossed her arms, turning toward the open door. "You should go with her. To Chicago."

Andri sputtered. "Wait. You're serious? I—"

Tabby shut the door and sat on the edge of his bed. "I heard the doctor, Andri. There's a good chance you'll limp the rest of your life. You might even need a cane. Can you be a policeman with such an injury?"

Andri's jaw clenched. He hadn't wanted to think about it, but the fact was, his career was over. Even if it wasn't, he wouldn't be able to return to full duty for months.

"There's nothing keeping you here, Andri, especially if she's there. And before you protest, you can't ask her to leave her job."

Andri shook his head. He wouldn't make her choose.

Tabby cleared her throat. "She doesn't know I overheard her conversation with her boss. She loves her job, Andri, and I think she's good at it."

"You're right."

This time, Tabby sputtered.

Andri grinned. "Your attitude has changed, too. You wouldn't want to go to Chicago now, would you?"

Her eyes widened. "If you went, Ma and Pa might let me."

His baby sister wasn't a baby anymore. This poised woman talking to him about relationships and adult matters was no child. "One step at a time, huh?"

Tabby nodded. "Oh, Gabby said she's expecting a colleague. Emma Hancock. She's a sports journalist, I guess. Goes to all the baseball games in Chicago and travels to all the big sporting events."

"Like that, do you?" He smiled at her excitement. Yes, his sister had caught the journalist bug, if that's what it was. "Do you think Gabby would ... could ... well—"

"You want to see her." Tabby patted his shoulder as she stood, and winked. "I'll send her in, just leave the door open."

"Shoo!" Andri felt his face turn red. Tabby laughed.

As he waited for Gabby, he pushed fingers through his hair, straightened his shirt, and ensured he was covered modestly despite his wrapped and cushioned leg being on display.

"Hey." Gabby appeared in the doorway, arms hugging her drawing pad. Freya leaned against her.

"Here's a chair so you can remain proper." Tabby nudged Gabby and Freya into the room with the front of the chair, which she then placed beside Andri's bed. "I'll be listening, so behave."

"She's enjoying this entirely too much," Andri muttered.

The humor didn't work. Gabby perched on the edge of the chair, still holding the drawing pad like a shield. Her gaze stayed pinned on his hairy leg, giving him the urge to hide the limb.

"Gabby, talk to me?" He held out his hand, not that he could reach her.

Freya tucked herself under the chair, lying on the rug that usually served as her bed.

"I have a confession, Andri." Still she didn't look at him. "First, I want you to look at two sketches and tell me if you recognize either of them."

Her serious tone sparked a whole new set of worries. And a confession? "Alright. Do you have the sketches with you?"

She nodded, then handed him her pad. "That's the first,

then flip the page up to see the second."

Andri studied the first sketch. The person wore a knit hat covering his hair, forehead, and ears. A piece of fabric covered his nose and mouth. With a coat buttoned up under the chin, there wasn't much to identify the person.

He flipped to the second image. This one had more detail and one notable difference between it and the first. He tapped the second image. "This is definitely a man. The broad face and muscular neck. Even with the hat covering what I would guess to be short hair."

"He isn't clean shaven, either." Gabriella scooted back in her chair. "What else?"

"This isn't the man from the boat last night. Cook, right? The man who I had to threaten over the telephone."

Gabby nodded, her cheeks darkening. "Once Emma arrives, I'd like to see if I can find where he and Molly went. The island isn't that big, so there must be a trail."

"I wish I could go along." Andri dropped his chin. "You know, this could be my attacker."

"You think so?" Gabby sat on the edge of the bed and Andri turned the sketch so she could see it without being uncomfortable.

"He had the same broad shoulders. Remember how I said that Cook didn't have the right build? This is the right build." Andri tilted his head to catch Gabby's gaze. "Who is this?"

She stared at the paper. "The man who killed Billy."

"So he thinks I'm investigating Holland's murder?" Dread slipped down his spine. "And he knows you're here."

"But you aren't investigating and he didn't come after me last night." Gabby hugged her middle. "And doesn't it seem suspicious that Thomas Cook and Molly arrived the same night this man attacked you?"

"You think they're linked."

"Billy and I planned to talk about those two before he was ... killed." She chewed her lip for a moment. "What about the first sketch?"

He turned back to it. "If the second image is your eyewitness sketch of Holland's murderer, who is this?"

"Not yet. First I need your impressions."

"Now that I've seen the second image, I can't help comparing them. What I noticed first when I flipped to the second image was how obvious it was that the second person was male. Could this first person be female?"

Gabby froze. She didn't blink. Andri wasn't even sure she drew in a breath. Slowly color leached from her face and something like fear grew in her eyes.

"Who is this, Gabby?" How he wished he could move. Hold her. Comfort her.

"There's a lady walking up the drive." Tabby appeared in the doorway.

Gabby flinched as Freya scrambled out from under her chair.

"Let Freya greet the visitor." He trusted his dog's instinct to know if the person could be hostile.

Tabby glanced at Gabby, then nodded. This time, she closed the door after Freya.

"Gabby, talk to me. Please." Andri set the sketch aside and tried to twist toward her, but the pain that shot through his leg wouldn't allow him. "Who is the person in the sketch?"

"The person who killed my mother."

Twenty-Five

Gabriella couldn't breathe. Why had she never considered that her mother's murderer could be a female? She had unwittingly eliminated half of all suspects.

Did Chief Michelsen suspect the person's gender? Why hadn't he said anything? Is that why he never wanted her to draw the sketch? Did he know more than he would admit?

"Gabby?" Andri's voice reached her like a warm breeze. If only she didn't feel locked in a block of ice, she could respond. Why hadn't she confided in him earlier?

Because of the kiss.

Freya barked. That had to be Emma. She needed to greet her friend and colleague, except she still couldn't get her limbs to move.

"Gabby, don't make me move, please." Andri's desperation cracked the ice and she managed to lift her head. His eyes pleaded with her to let him help.

She leaned forward so he could grasp her hand without jostling his leg. "I first sketched that image the morning of my mother's funeral. Chief Michelsen forbade me from telling anyone. I ... I ..."

Andri tugged her fingers so she had to look at him again. "You witnessed your mother's murder."

Gabby nodded as tears tripped down her cheeks. She brushed them away with the back of her free hand. "That person doesn't know. At least, I don't think so. That was the reason the chief wouldn't let me say anything. But I would have told you."

"If I hadn't butchered our friendship." Andri flopped against his pillows and released a massive breath. "I knew I was a fool, but wow. Gabby, how could you ever trust me again?"

"That's the funny thing." She traced her thumb carefully around the broken skin along his knuckles. "I never stopped trusting you. I thought the mistake was mine, that I was the reason for our friendship breaking. You saw me as a little sister, so I determined to be exactly that."

"But this secret, you couldn't tell me." He patted the

drawing pad.

Female voices and the excited padding of Freya's paws indicated their time was short. Urgency thawed the rest of the ice that had bound her. "I couldn't until yesterday, it's true. Forgive me, Andri? Please. I never meant to hurt you."

"There is nothing to forgive, Gabby. I—"

"Andri? Gabby?" Tabby's sing-song greeting preceded her entrance into the room. "Emma Hancock has arrived and insisted on speaking with Gabby at once."

Relief at seeing Emma propelled her forward. Emma chuckled as she returned the hug.

"I am sure I'm as dirty as an outfielder. What a drive that is, and I left only an hour after you called Ali." Emma's voice danced like fireflies on a summer night. She pulled back to grip Gabriella's shoulders. "Let me see you. Ali made me promise a thorough report."

Gabriella bore the scrutiny by doing her own assessment. Emma wore a mauve fascinator at a jaunty angle over brown wavy hair, the lace and flowers declaring her feminine side. Her matching wool coat outlined a trim, athletic figure from shoulders to shins, and serviceable black lace-up boots completed the look.

"You need sleep." Emma shrugged. "But when do we ever get enough when a story is unfolding? Tabby is a peach. Now introduce me to her brother, won't you?"

Gabriella laughed. That was Emma. Feminine and direct. "This is Andri. Andri, meet Emma Hancock of the Di Stasio Giornaliste Agency."

"A pleasure to meet one of Gabby's colleagues." Andri dipped his head in greeting.

"My, he's a polite one." Emma widened her eyes at Gabriella, then swept forward with all the flourish of a performer. "The pleasure is mine. I bring our boss's gratitude for keeping our Gabriella safe. And, we are sorry to hear of your injury. Knee, is it? Which way did it bend?"

"Emma!" Gabriella hissed.

"What? There are multiple knee ligaments that can sustain damage. Did you know, this Swiss doc, Bircher, actually opened the knee to repair the damage? Or wait, was it the Italian surgeon, Putti, who repaired the torn ligament? Anyway, that is all in the last ten years. Imagine—"

"And all in Europe, Em." Gabriella shook her head.

Emma waved away the thought. "Athletes are always looking for ways to repair an injury so it won't cost them their career. Why would it be different for a policeman?"

Silence reigned.

Emma shrugged once again, using the motion to remove her coat. "Now, Ali sent me with documents and news.

I assume your policeman would like to hear my report, Gabriella, or is the info all for you?"

"I'll go make myself scarce." Tabby sighed. "Come on, Freya."

"Tabby, wait," Andri called after her. "Stay. If you want to be a journalist, you could learn something from these two."

"Really?" Tabby breathed.

"If that's alright?" This question he directed toward Emma and Gabriella.

Emma raised a brow at Gabriella. "Are you recruiting or training your replacement?"

"Recruiting." Andri spoke before Gabriella could think of what to say.

Gabriella's heart lurched. She stared at Andri, daring to read between his words. He gave a small nod and tears stung her nose. She looked up at the ceiling to keep her emotions in check. Andri wanted to come to Chicago with her, and wanted her to continue to be a journalist. Could she do both? Like Ali, be a journalist and a ... wife?

"You two can finish your relationship conversation later." Emma laid her coat on the dresser, took Gabriella's seat, and set her satchel on the bed. "We have multiple angles and persons of interest. Carrie provided quite a bit of this information."

"Who is Carrie?" Andri asked as he patted the bed beside him.

Gabriella sat on the edge of the mattress, highly uncomfortable even though Tabby also sat on the bed near his feet. "Uh, Carrie Wagoneer is an undercover investigative journalist. She's been hunting down corrupt cops of late."

"Which is how we knew Detective Arthur was one of the good ones." Emma removed a folder. "He provided this. Carrie also believes Officer Wilson is clean, but is cautious that he could be corruptible if the right skirt flashed his way."

"You are really blunt." Andri's face was as red as the streaks in his hair.

"Why hide the truth? Making something ugly look pretty does everyone a disservice." Emma removed another file. "Lena and Griff have information on Cook and Molly Zander, but I doubt it's anything you haven't already discovered, Gabriella."

"Cook's womanizing makes Officer Wilson's flirting look like a boy's first crush." Gabriella opened Lena's file. "Molly, though. I need to find out why she's on the island. She and I have never spoken, and quite honestly, I can't imagine she would even know who I am."

Andri took Carrie's file. "About that ... I've been

thinking about how Cook arrived on the island. It was similar to how those barrels arrived the night you called me."

"I called you." Gabriella stared at Andri, memories snapping into place, of telling the operator where to transfer her call that night. "Thomas Cook knows you live here, thinks you're my beau. If I disappeared, wouldn't he think I came here?"

"He wasn't my attacker, though."

"And it doesn't account for Molly's presence," Emma added.

"I might have a way to find out." Tabby spoke up. "Emma is a stranger here, so she would be noticed. Gabriella is the one in danger, so she needs to stay here. Andri isn't allowed off this bed. But I can go to town."

Andri was shaking his head, but Gabriella jumped in before he could speak. "You realize the danger you could put yourself in?"

Emma leveled a look at Tabby. "Can you defend yourself if you're caught somewhere they don't want you?"

"I don't know. I only know what my family thinks of me, that I flaunt the rules when I'm simply earning a few extra dollars. Mr. Kristensen said I'm good at numbers. I've simply been analyzing the cost of wheat and corn and milk and its effect on what he stocks in the store. Figures make sense to me."

"That's what you've been doing?" Andri sat up with a wince. "Why haven't you told us?"

Tabby rolled her eyes. "Why do you think? All I'm expected to do is find a husband. I do want to get married someday, and what man is going to want a woman who knows the cost of pork?"

Andri laid his large hand over Gabriella's. "He has to be out there. You three are some of the most intelligent women I've met, and I wouldn't change a thing about you. I only want you safe." His chin dropped to his chest.

"I know, Brother. I'll have Emma give me a few tips before I head to town."

"A brilliant plan." Emma rose, then slid the last folder toward Gabriella. "From Ali. You need to read this."

Emma closed the door behind her and Tabby, leaving Gabriella alone with Andri and Freya. Her fingers shook as she opened the folder.

Twenty-Six

Andri braced for what Gabby would reveal in this last folder.

"Ali has been gathering information on my mother's murder." Gabby lifted a news article, then a page of handwritten notes. "Looks like she started investigating the same week I joined the agency."

"Is that good?" Andri took the new article from her. It was a simple story about her mother's death, nothing he didn't already know. "Did she find anything new?"

She didn't appear to hear him. "I thought it a boon to find a fellow Italian to work for, but she's been so much more. She's our defender, our encourager, our leader."

"I look forward to meeting her." Despite his knee and the uncertainty it should bring, the last hours had brought undeniable clarity. He would go to Chicago with Gabby, men left for the city to find work all the time. And he had a feeling Ali could help.

"It looks like she's been in contact with Chief Michelsen over the years." Gabby frowned. "I wonder why neither ever told me."

He'd like to know the answer to that, too. "Why didn't the chief want you to investigate?"

"To protect me. I'm the only eyewitness. If no one knew that, then I was safe. But look at that sketch, Andri. How can that identify someone?"

He held up a finger and called for Emma.

Freya raised her head and a moment later Emma entered the room. "Your sister has just left. She's a smart one. I'd like to introduce her to Ali. I think she'd make a crack reporter. Now what can I do for you two?"

Andri tucked Emma's opinion of Tabby away and opened Gabby's sketches to the one of her mother's murderer, handing it to Emma. "How good are you recognizing someone beneath a mask?"

Emma's eyes sparked. "I report on athletics. In gear they often look nothing like they do every day. Who is this?"

Andri guessed as much. "I need you to go down to Lydia's Kitchen to get us a loaf of her Surdeigsbrød. She closes soon, so you'll want to stop there first. Then go by

Joel's Diner to get a crock of his soup of the day."

"What are you playing at, Andri?" Gabby asked. "This isn't about a meal. Aunt Deb will bring supper tonight."

"You want me to look for this person." Emma studied the sketch. "What do I need to know?"

"They are potentially very dangerous." Andri tucked the news article into the folder Ali had sent. "Is that enough information?"

"Gabriella?" Emma handed her the sketch pad. "Anything else?"

Andri hid a smile. Yes, these women were strong, fierce even. He admired them, even as he feared for their safety. Even Emma, whom he had only just met.

She shook her head. "I don't want to bias you."

Emma nodded. "You should get Andri another snow pack and let him rest. Then take time to draw. We shared a lot of information just now and I know you. Let it congeal."

"Sound plan." Andri gathered the file folders, noting how correct Emma was in her assessment. He was tired, and his knee ached something fierce. All the conversation had helped him ignore it, but it wouldn't be ignored for much longer. "Emma? Be careful, will you?"

Emma tipped an imaginary hat, and was soon out the front door.

Gabby lingered, her features scrunched in concentration.

"What is it?" Andri handed her the files and she hugged them to her chest.

"I can't pin it down. Like that day in Joel's diner, or in Billy's room, there is something I'm missing."

"Then do as Emma suggested. Go draw. Take Freya with you, make a cup of coffee. I've watched you each morning since you arrived, you know. That's what you need to do right now."

She gathered her belongings and headed for the door. Paused. "I never thought you approved of me being a journalist."

Andri's shoulders dropped. "I'm sorry, Gabby."

"Why?" Her brown eyes were large in her round face as she glanced over her shoulder. "Why the change now?"

"Because I didn't understand." He scrubbed the uninjured side of his jaw. "Because ... because I couldn't be there to protect you. I'm not proud of it, Gabby, but helplessness made me a boar. I'm sorry."

"I always knew I could count on you, Andri."

"You still ..." His gaze drifted to his knee. Could he be the protector she needed when he couldn't walk?

"Yes, I still can and I still do." Gabriella tapped her thigh for Freya to follow her. "Try not to worry. I'll just be at the kitchen table."

After Gabby got him settled with a new cold pack around his knee, Andri settled in to. He was just drifting off when a light knock came at his door..

"Gabby?" Andri opened one eye.

"You were sleeping." She ducked. "I'll—"

"Wait." He wouldn't go back to sleep until he knew why she'd checked on him. "What is it? Tell me."

Instead of the smile he expected, her eyes turned glassy. "Do you think it is alright if I sit in here with you? Even though we've sent both our chaperones on errands?"

He had two choices, discover why she desired to sit here with him or chase down why she worried about chaperones. The first would be the wiser, more professional choice, but it was one he could return to. The second offered him an opportunity he was loathe to give up.

He relaxed in his pillows. "Why would you worry about a chaperone? It makes no difference if you are in here or out there. We still have none."

Freya brushed past Gabby's legs, swishing her skirt. Gabby leaned into the doorjamb. "I don't want you to feel uncomfortable."

He narrowed his gaze, assessing the truth behind her words. "What about your discomfort?"

She shrugged.

"Nope. I need an answer, Gabby." He scrutinized her, the shy tilt of her head, the protective hold on her drawing pad, the pink ... "Are you so used to men assuming your reputation is tawdry that you don't even defend it?"

"I trust you, Andri." She straightened. "I always have. I've never worried for myself when around you, but lately ... Well, you're right about how other men see me. If that bothers you, I want to give you an escape."

He didn't quite believe her. Yes, there was a nugget of truth in her words, but there was more to it. "You didn't worry about that when you arrived."

"I thought you saw me as a little sister." She plopped into the chair that had remained at his bedside. "These sketches, Andri. I've always said my curiosity would kill me one day, but now I fear that phrase may be less idiom and more prophetic truth."

Ah, now they were getting somewhere. He'd always worried her curiosity would get her into trouble, too, but he wouldn't confirm that fear now. "Can you tell me why?"

"It's one thing to connect people, draw them, then hand the investigative part over to a journalist like Billy or Ali or Carrie. I've dreamed of doing what Ali and Carrie do, but now that I'm here, staring at these faces I sketched, it's a frightful thing." Her voice dropped with each word, her pencil held by unsteady fingers. "One or more of these people wish me harm. Or you."

This was about him? "You don't have to worry ..." A glance at his knee cut off the ridiculous platitude. She had every reason to worry about him.

"I'm frozen, Andri." She hugged her drawing pad again. "If I draw, I could bring danger. If I don't draw, justice won't be served. I'm the eyewitness. I can identify the man who murdered Billy, the person who killed ..."

"Gabby, love, stop." How he wished he could leap out of this bed. "Do you know why I became a policeman?"

She blinked away the droplets on her lashes and shook her head.

"After you left the island, I left, too. I couldn't forgive myself for the way I hurt you. I thought, if I could find the person who killed your mother, perhaps I could face you again."

Her brows scrunched together.

"So I went looking, got myself embedded in a couple smuggling routes, until a Prohibition agent straightened me out. He sponsored me to become a police officer, and I went undercover a couple times for him. That wasn't his end goal, though. He talked about justice and what it really meant."

Gabby tilted her head.

"Justice is a legal term describing how to judge moral and fair behavior. I wanted the people who hurt you to get their just desserts, but that isn't justice. What I wanted was revenge. What those people did to your mom, to Holland, it was and is immoral and deserves punishment, but who am I to mete out that punishment?"

"Ali talks about that, too. How we, as journalists, uncover the unjust ways of humans, but it is not our job to punish. Only to reveal."

"And as a policeman, my job is similar. I stand between the innocent and anyone who would do them harm. I collect evidence of unjust behavior. But I am not the judge. I am not the one who pronounces judgment. And I realized, thanks to my friend, that I did not want that responsibility on my shoulders. I am too imperfect. Protecting the innocent is where I belong."

"You're good at that, Andri."

He didn't let her kind words derail his point. "You are one of these innocents, Gabby. And the way I feel about you makes me even more protective of you. I know that means I can be overbearing. I know this knee puts me at a disadvantage. But it doesn't mean I won't try, even if I might fail. I'm trained to do this. Can you trust me to protect you as much as I can?"

Her brown eyes turned glassy once again. "But if I wasn't an eyewitness—"

"None of this is your fault. You are not the one who damaged my knee."

She hiccuped a sob, driving a piling deep into his being. Did these women, these strong-hearted journalists, have someone protecting them? Someone giving them a sense of security so they could do the job only they could do? Who looked out for their physical protection so they could shed light in the darkness?

He let the questions gather in his chest, but focused on the present, on soothing her worries. "Gabby, between Freya's ear and the pistol at my side, we'll be safe. Concentrate on your sketches. We need you. I'll even close my eyes again so you don't wonder if I'm looking over your shoulder."

The emotion that bound her smoothed out in her expression and she sniffed as she dashed away the tears that fell. "Yes, yes, I appreciate that. Thanks, Andri."

His heart soared and he closed his eyes. Well, mostly closed them. Through the slits, he surreptitiously watched her work. Never had he seen a more beautiful woman.

Twenty-Seven

Gabriella's pencil flew over the paper, creating drawing after drawing.

For the first time since Billy died, or perhaps from even before then, she didn't censor herself. She allowed her trust in Andri to free her intuition. The result was astonishing. Never had she drawn with such detail, or remembered scenes so clearly.

Her room, Billy's room, the face of his murderer. Joel's diner, his kitchen, office, and safe. Her parents, then her mother. Tears dripped onto the page as she drew, for the first time, Mama's death.

Freya pressed her nose onto her lap, upending her sketch pad. She glanced up to discover Andri sitting on the edge of the bed.

"Andri! Your leg."

He snagged a blanket to cover the bare limb. The doctor had sliced the fabric from his trousers, and he'd not changed them. His cotton shirt was untucked, the button loose at his throat. Her gaze stalled on the breadth of muscle across his chest.

Warmth spread through her. She hadn't fully comprehended the impropriety of being alone with him, here in his room, until this moment. He'd been in bed, hurt, in need of help, but that wasn't the impression he gave now.

No, now an intense glint shone from his eyes. "You are crying."

She bit her lip and dashed the offending drops from her cheeks.

"What memory have you drawn?" He leaned toward her, balancing his weight with this good leg, tugging the drawing pad free.

She stayed silent, the sketch was obvious. Instead, she watched the tendons in his face, his neck, his shoulders. The way they tensed to bands of steel as emotion gripped him.

He tapped his thumb on the murderer's body. "Smaller frame than my attacker. Did we send Emma on a goose chase? What is the probability your mother's murderer is still on the island?"

"She will make sure of that the best she can." Gabriella took back the drawing pad, trying to regain her equilibrium.

Freya plopped onto the rug, but Andri didn't settle back on the bed. If anything, his intensity grew.

"As much as I want to see justice for my mama, I think we need to choose one problem at a time." She turned the pages to the sketch of Billy's room, desperate to calm the nerves crawling along her skin. "Most pressing is Billy's murder and your attack. We think they are perpetrated by the same person, which may have something to do with why Cook and Molly are on the island."

Andri hummed. "Slide your chair closer so you can show me the sketches."

She obliged, wanting to make it easier for him, but was surprised when Andri rested his arm on the back of her chair. If she turned her head, he would be near enough to kiss. "This is distracting."

"Is it?" His chuckle warmed her ear.

She gasped and shot a quick glance at him. "I didn't mean to say that out loud."

Her words faded to nothing as he held her gaze with his own. A confusing mix of tension and excitement churned in her stomach. Andri cupped her cheek, and ran his thumb over her cheekbone.

Usually, when a man hemmed her in, especially as Andri did now—large body hovering, one arm behind her, other hand guiding her face closer—she would have yelled, screamed, done anything to get away. Sure, her heart pounded, but not with fear.

Nope. Not at all.

Her eyes drifted closed. His lips caressed hers in a kiss even more treasured than the one by the lighthouse.

"I love you, Gabby." Another feather-light kiss. "I love your heart for justice, your compassion, your wisdom, your fierceness, your shyness, everything about you."

Freya's nose slipped between them.

"My intention, Gabriella Salatino, if you'll allow me, is to court you properly." A third kiss, a fourth. "I want to show you how much I love you. And then, perhaps, I can convince you to be my wife."

"What." The word rushed out in a breath and her eyes snapped open.

Andri pulled back with a nod. "I mean it, Gabby. I plan to follow you to Chicago, meet Ali and your colleagues, prove to you and them that I am worthy of you."

"You have nothing to prove. I—"

Freya's bark made her jump. Her pencil and sketch pad tumbled to the floor as Freya scrambled out the bedroom door.

"Someone's here." Andri pulled his pistol from the holster on his bed. "Stay here."

"How will you walk?" Gabby searched the room for something he could use as a walking stick, knowing he wouldn't let her go with him. "Use the chair."

He agreed and Gabriella stood in the doorway, using the door as a shield as she watched Andri limp his way after Freya and praying for his protection. Four of his halting steps and he stopped, glancing back at her, and she realized Freya had stopped barking. An eerie quiet infiltrated the house.

"Hello, it's just Emma here!" Her friend's voice carried down the hall and fear shot through Gabriella. That was the distress code Ali taught them.

"Andri, stop," she hissed. He hadn't turned the corner to be in full sight of the front door and she made sure to stay back. "She's under duress."

Andri leaned on the chair back, jaw hard. "You sure?"

She nodded.

"Go up to the attic," he whispered. "Take down the picture and pull the logs out. Every house needs two escape routes. Take your sketches and get help."

"Gabby?" Emma's singsong tone set her on edge, as her friend never called her that nickname.

"Go. Please." The crack in Andri's voice had her spinning for the satchel she'd left on the kitchen table. She tucked her sketchpad inside and climbed up the ladder to the loft, even as her heart cracked at the danger she left Andri and Emma to face alone.

"Oh, Andri." Emma's false cheer wavered. "You're up and moving."

"Where's the other girl?" That voice belonged to Billy's murderer. Gabriella shivered and climbed faster.

Everything in her wanted to stay, to fight. But Emma knew how to protect herself, and Andri was armed. Apparently, Gabriella was the one the man wanted, so she needed to get far away from here. And trust Andri's directions.

She spotted the picture Andri mentioned and stumbled. It was one she'd drawn for him before her mother died. A lighthouse at sunset. It had no color, being only a sketch, but it had been a gift for him during the last Christmas they'd spent together.

He'd not only kept it, he used it as a sign of rescue, of escape.

She lifted down the frame, noticed the notch in the wood of the wall. Tucking her fingers into the space, she pulled. The log that came out was heavy and thumped onto the floor once she got it free.

Afternoon sunlight filled the attic. Commotion sounded downstairs. Gabriella climbed through the hole, maneuvered so that she hung from the opening, then dropped the many feet to hard ground. She rolled as Ali had daughter her—it paid to have a boss who had once been a street urchin, adept at evading the police.

Gaining her feet, she ran toward town, hoping, praying, begging God to protect Andri and Emma and Freya. And deliver justice for Billy.

Twenty-Eight

Andri could put no weight on his leg, leaving him unable to move without leaning heavily on the chair back. But going back wasn't an option. As he listened for Gabby's escape up to the loft, he hid his pistol at his side and inched toward the front door.

"Oh, Andri, you're up and moving." Emma tilted her head and mouthed, *Is she safe?*

He did not acknowledge her as the person with her drew his attention. "Where's the other girl?" A well-built man pushed through the front door, a revolver pointed at Emma's head. He had the same clothing style and body type as the man from Gabby's sketch, the one who murdered Billy.

"I suppose I have you to thank for my knee." Andri

shuffled forward, analyzing, planning ... How could he take down this murderer? "Where's my dog?"

The man sneered. "I was going to shoot it, but the girl took my rope and said she knew how to disable the dog without a sound."

As if Emma would help him. Andri could see the irritation in her eyes at the implication, though she quickly blinked it away. "She's hogtied and muzzled on the porch." *But alive.*

Freya might be injured, even traumatized because of this treatment, but she'd live. He had to be all right with that. For now.

"Now what?" Andri shifted forward, his knee nearly buckling. He forced the pain back and cocked an ear for Gabby's movement. He would stall until he was sure she'd gotten away, unless Emma's life was in immediate danger. Then ... well, hopefully a plan would come to mind.

"Now?" He pressed his weapon against Emma's head. Her mouth pressed into a firm line. "You hand over—"

A crash reverberated from the loft.

The man jumped, his gun shifting from Emma's head. With a spark of inspiration, Andri fired his pistol at the wall and the man leveled his gun at him instead of Emma.

Emma sent a back kick into the man's stomach, knocking him into the door. The woman had skill. Andri pushed the chair toward her and she swung it at the man's head, connecting with a solid crack. The man dropped and Emma hit him again with the chair.

"Don't move." Andri grabbed hold of an umbrella from the coat tree to support his weight as he limped forward, pistol trained on the man. "Stand down, Emma."

"Toss me that scarf." She pointed to the coat tree. "I'll tie him like he made me tie Freya."

Andri obliged. The pain in his knee was rapidly depleting his energy, obvious from the way tossing a scarf took too much concentration. "Can you slide that chair back over?" He had to keep up his strength. This wasn't over.

"Happily." Emma tugged the knot she'd made with the scarf before pushing the chair in his direction. "I'll get Freya and use her ropes to muzzle this animal. Harming innocent dogs. Heinous."

A smile fought for release as he eased his bulk into the chair. "You do know he's knocked out and can't hear you." Though Andri didn't relax his aim in case the man woke or was feigning unconsciousness.

"It makes me feel better." Emma glared at the man who lay on his side, blood trickling from a gash in his temple. "I don't kick a man while he's down, but I admit to being tempted. He tossed me about and I don't let anyone do such a thing."

"Emma?" He drew her attention. "Freya."

She yanked open the front door and Andri tried not to close his eyes. Exhaustion and pain battled hard, but he couldn't let down his guard.

Gratefulness for Emma's presence filled him. The woman had history with a man like this murderer here. It was the only explanation for such an emotional response. But she was strong, determined. It didn't surprise him that she and Gabby were friends. Both women would be good influences on Tabby, too.

The man on the ground shifted, showing signs of waking. They'd get some answers, then deliver him to town. Unless Gabby returned with help first.

Please let her stay safe.

Freya barked and a moment later barreled inside, leaping over the man on the floor to race to Andri's side.

"There's my good girl." Andri rubbed her flank. "You alright?"

Freya's tail swished.

"I'm sorry, Andri. Your dog didn't deserve that." Emma knelt beside the man and used the ropes to secure him, eliciting a groan from him in response to her rough treatment. "It was the only way I could think of to keep her alive."

"I know." Andri scratched Freya's ears. "I think she knows, too. She let you muzzle her without biting you."

Emma snatched a hat from the coat rack to gag their prisoner. "Do you think she knew I was protecting her?"

"She's a smart one." Andri smiled. "And we gave Gabby a chance to escape."

"Where did she go? I don't know this man's name, but Henchman here is only a lackey. Muscle."

Henchman swung his legs at Emma's feet and she hopped out of the way. In an instant, Freya stood over the man with bared teeth.

"You know who he works for?" Andri let his pistol rest on his thigh, ready, if needed, but Freya had the matter in hand.

"I don't have the proof Ali would require before printing a story, but I'm confident enough to offer a tip to the police. It's the same person as one of the sketches you showed me." Emma watched their prisoner and Freya. "That first place you sent me, the kitchen. It's the lady who owns it."

"Miss Lydia?"

Emma shrugged. "Same build, same face structure. And I'm pretty sure she uses coloring in her hair to make her look older."

"How would you know that?"

"I used to act." Emma waved away the question. "Does anyone know Gabriella drew that sketch?"

"Just the chief." Did that mean …? "We need to get to town. You said this man works for Lydia?"

"They spoke together before he followed me." Emma hesitated. "How much do you know about this Lydia?"

"Why?" Andri demanded.

Freya growled low in her throat. Henchmen was trying to move again.

"Because she has the same bone structure as Molly."

"What are you saying?" Andri used the coat tree to pull himself to his feet. "That they're sisters? Relatives? What?"

"Molly is our age." Emma rubbed her forehead. "No one knows anything about her mother. Her father is a ruthless businessman, so it's no wonder she's acquainted with Thomas Cook."

"You think Lydia is Molly's mother? As in, the woman who possibly killed Gabby's mother?"

"She what?" Emma gaped. "That's what the last file was about, wasn't it? Ali designated that one for Gabriella's eyes only."

"Do you think Henchman knows more?" Andri adjusted his grip on the umbrella he used as a cane. Rational thought evaded him. He wanted to run to Gabby's rescue, but if Henchman had information that could help them, he had to extract it now.

"Not worth the time." Emma rested her hand on Andri's arm. "If this is true, then we need to get to town right now. We'll find people faster than dealing with telephone operators."

Andri's pulse picked up speed.

"I'll secure him here so you can properly arrest him later." She squeezed his arm. "We will protect her."

Together, they secured Henchman to the kitchen table leg, then Emma helped Andri out to the automobile she'd driven up from Chicago, Freya following on their heels. He had no protest when she insisted she drive them to town. His knee ached something horrible.

The road to town was a narrow, rocky path that jarred the car, especially with the speed with which Emma drove. Andri clenched his teeth against the pain. He'd manage if it meant reaching Gabby that much quicker.

The car bounced onto the brick-paved road of Main Street proper. Another moment, and Emma careened to a stop outside the jailhouse.

She glanced over at him and cringed. "Sorry about my driving. Did you want to speak to the chief before we track down Gabriella?"

"Help me out, would you?" He needed fresh air or the pain might have him casting up what little he'd eaten today.

Emma had barely helped him to his feet when Joel charged toward them. Freya leaped to Andri's side and Emma stepped in front of them, not that she blocked much of him, being so slender and him so large. Still. Brave, selfless women, these journalists. Gabby fit right in.

"This was in my office." Joel brandished an iron paperweight shaped like a cannon. "It's not mine. Could the thief have left it? I don't remember it there the other day."

Emma stepped aside, meeting Andri's gaze with a glance at the pistol holstered at his belt.

Andri rested his palm on it, more to keep Emma from taking it than because of Joel. "You sure it's not yours?"

"What's going on?" Joel looked between the two of them, then at Andri's knee.

"That's Billy Holland's." Emma jabbed her chin at the paperweight. "Taken from the scene of his murder."

"Only, we know Joel wasn't there." Andri stepped in before Emma disabled Jakobsen. "He's been set up. We need to find Gabby. Now."

"What's going on?" Joel pocketed the paperweight. "Gabriella just walked into Lydia's Kitchen with Tabby."

Andri's stomach turned.

If only he could run.

TWENTY-NINE

Gabriella stopped abruptly within the doorway of Lydia's Kitchen.

Tabby bumped her from behind. "What is it?"

When Gabriella had arrived at the jailhouse in search of Chief Michelsen, she'd found it empty. Out of breath from running to town, desperate to find someone to help Andri and Emma, she wasn't proud of the fact it had caused her a moment of indecision. But before she'd been able to decide where to find help next, Tabby showed up with news that Chief Michelsen was here at Lydia's Kitchen. Gabriella had surged into action again.

"Gabby?" Tabby's voice shook in Gabriella's ear, snapping her back to her present moment.

Of the scenarios Gabriella could have imagined she'd

find when tracking down Chief Michelsen, walking into a room to see Molly Zander pointing a gun at her wasn't one of them.

"Put the weapon down, Molly," Chief Michelsen ordered, but did not intervene. He stood beside Lydia near the doorway to the kitchen, making no move to ensure Gabriella's safety.

"I don't think so." Molly waved the pistol. "Slide the bolt on that door."

Gabriella hesitated, still trying to wrap her mind around the scene. No other patrons were in the place, except Thomas Cook, who stood passively by. That didn't surprise her. But Chief Michelsen?

The click of a lock jolted her to the present. Tabby had obeyed, had locked them inside. Gabby's thoughts misfired. Was Tabby part of this? Did she lie about staying late to work at Kristensen's? Could she be an accomplice to ... whatever this was?

"Sit here." Molly pointed to a table in the center of the room.

Not happening. Gabriella knew better than to get close to a person waving a weapon around like it was a cigarette holder. She looked to the chief, hoping he'd have a way out. He merely nodded to the chair. Tabby nudged her forward.

No! She had to find her tongue. Her curiosity wouldn't kill her this time. She'd use it as a weapon. Buy time for—

"Sit," Molly commanded, the deadness in her eyes chilling Gabriella worse than a northeast wind off Lake Superior.

"Molly, you've scared the poor girl." Thomas rolled his eyes, but remained leaning against the left wall. "She might not know you've sent your man to dispense with her beau."

Tabby gasped. Gabriella's jaw tightened.

"Apparently she knows." Molly glared at her, calculating, conniving. "But she doesn't—"

Something heavy rammed into the door behind them. Gabriella spun. A bullet slammed into the doorframe beside her and Tabby screamed.

"Gabby!" Andri?

"I said sit down." Molly fired again, hitting the same spot on the wall.

The pounding on the door increased, accompanied by jiggling and male voices. Gabriella turned slowly, no longer frightened by Molly's show. If the woman meant to kill her, she would have done it just then.

"We need to listen to her." Tabby tugged Gabriella's arm. Was the young woman on Molly's side? Gabriella studied Chief Michelsen more closely. Was he?

The chief subtly inclined his head toward Lydia and shifted to his left, revealing the glint of a knife, which Lydia held to his side.

"Gabby." Tabby's voice shook. Ah, the girl wasn't on Molly's side ... She was just scared to death and trying desperately to hide it. "She's going to shoot us."

"No, she's not." Gabriella met Molly's gaze, more pieces clicking into place. She let her curiosity take control with a bit of calculated fishing. "Because then she wouldn't get to find out how much the authorities know about her smuggling ring."

Lydia's quick inhalation drew Gabriella's attention. Chief Michelsen subtly shook his head. How much had he figured out? Is that why he'd kept Andri away? She needed more information, and she needed to buy Andri time to find a way inside.

Molly swore, mixing in an Italian slur. "I'll motivate you in a different way, since I don't need the blonde." She shifted her aim toward Tabby.

Gabriella stepped in front of Andri's sister.

"This is ridiculous." Thomas marched forward. "Don't mar the beauty, Molly. Some of us appreciate that sort of thing. I'll take care of the blonde."

"Fine. Tie the girl to a chair and keep her quiet." Molly raised a perfectly arched brow, not taking her gaze from

Gabriella's. "And Mother, tie the chief to another chair while I take care of this witness."

Mother. Color washed over the image that her mind had pieced together. The smuggling, the cellar, the reason Molly had come to this island instead of any of the other places that would easily allow her to ship her illegal goods without resistance.

"Lydia is your mother." Gabby knew the words were inane, but air seemed in short supply as her mind whirred with the information.

"And she killed yours." Molly's smile chilled the room, sending ice into Gabriella's very bones.

For a moment, she heard nothing. Slowly, she became aware of the continual pounding at the door behind her, the scrape of chairs, the protests ... yet one thing remained. Deep in her soul, the purpose that had driven her. Justice. And Molly Zander had just confessed Lydia's crime.

"Neither of you will get away this time." Gabriella squared her shoulders, hand drifting to the satchel that hung at her side. "I'm an eyewitness, yes, but I'm also a journalist. I seek to illuminate the truth, to reveal the evil deeds so the innocent might find justice."

Molly snorted and Lydia, and even Cook, laughed. They'd relaxed, thinking they'd won. That Gabriella had allowed the truth to turn her into a spouting idiot.

Assuming the picture before them was all there was to see and the pounding at the door was all there was to hear.

But it wasn't.

As Gabriella freed her penknife from the pocket of her satchel, she spotted Freya crouched in the kitchen doorway. Behind her Emma had a bat in hand, which Gabriella knew she could wield. And Andri, leaning heavily on an umbrella, met her gaze, empowering her to see this through.

"See, Molly," Gabriella gripped the penknife, "a picture tells a tale, but it doesn't reveal the whole story. There's always more to it. The before and after. The motive. And so I suggest you lower your weapon. Your murderous smuggling is at an end."

Andri's command sent Freya for Lydia's arm before the woman could send her knife into Chief Michelsen's side. Molly turned and fired her weapon at Andri, but his own well-placed bullet unarmed her. As Emma secured Lydia, Gabriella unlocked the door and Joel tumbled inside.

Then an arm wrapped around her neck. "You assumed too much, darling."

The room stilled.

"You're not part of the ring, are you Mr. Cook?" Gabriella adjusted her grip on the penknife. "You came for me because you recognized the town where my *beau* lives.

Molly was your ticket, but I was your prize."

"Yes, Molly was useful, promised to eliminate your boyfriend," Cook snarled in her ear, "but I told you I always get what I want. So leave with me now and I won't—"

Gabriella slammed the blade of her penknife into his thigh.

The man howled, loosening his grip on her. In another moment, Joel had him in hand.

Andri limped his way toward Gabriella with single-minded focus, and Gabriella met him partway, letting him wrap her in his tight embrace.

"You're safe," he whispered into her hair, voice choked.

Gabriella nodded, squeezing her arms around his waist, never wanting to let go. "And so are you."

Then his lips were on hers in a kiss so full of relief it flooded her heart and she returned it in equal measure.

"Hey brother?" Tabby's laugh broke them apart. "The chief and I would like to be freed from these chairs. Then you lovebirds can kiss all you want."

"Humph." Chief Michelsen did a poor job of hiding his grin. "I knew he had kissing on the mind."

"Yes." Andri grinned down at Gabriella and she felt his love all the way down to her shoes. "I certainly do."

Freya barked or Gabriella was sure Andri would have

kissed her again, right then and there. A picture she wouldn't have minded sketching in the morning.

Thirty

Three days later, Andri eased himself out of a hansom cab in the heart of Chicago, his new cane assisting him. The ringing of bells from the church across the street momentarily distracted him before he could offer a hand to help Gabby, Tabby, then Emma alight. Freya bounded down after them.

"Everything is so ..." Tabby craned her neck, "tall and dirty and close and interesting."

"We aren't on Heima Island, that's for sure." Andri paid the driver after the man stacked their luggage on the ground beside them. "So this is home?"

Gabby slipped her arm through his free arm. "I don't think I realized how much it has become that, until now. Heima Island will still have a piece of my heart, but this is where I belong."

He heard the underlying message in her tone, in the way she kept her eyes on the Di Stasio building instead of on him. He kissed the side of her head. "Then it's where I belong, too."

"Ugh." Tabby groaned, snatching her carpetbag and marching up the steps to the building directly in front of them. "Please tell me I don't have to suffer one more minute of those two."

Emma laughed as she followed Tabby up the stairs, her bag in hand. "We can leave the lovebirds here, I'll introduce—"

The door of the building opened, revealing a curly-haired man with dark olive skin. His gaze rapidly took in the group, sparkling with good humor as he spotted Andri. "*Il tuo amore, Gabriella?*"

Did the man have to say her name with such beauty?

"This is Gio Vella." Emma bumped the man's arm. "A heartless matchmaker who has yet to find me a man willing to admit that a woman can play baseball."

Gio feigned a knife to the heart. "The pain, Emma. I look, but he is not in this great city."

"He's our best source," Gabby whispered to Andri. Interesting.

"I will get your luggage." Gio jogged down the steps,

Freya following him as if she'd met a new best friend. Figured.

"What is all the commotion?" A woman with red hair appeared with hands on her hips. "Is there a demonstration happening in the street?"

"Don't be ridiculous, Lena." A woman in a black skirt and white blouse nudged her out the door. "It appears our Gabriella has returned, safe and sound."

Gabby squeezed his arm, a look of pure pleasure encompassing her whole countenance. He wanted to have these introductions inside so he could rest his leg, but he could suffer a few minutes of pain to see that look on her face.

Emma wrapped her arm around Tabby's shoulders, backing everyone into the house so Gio could get by. "Gabby brought a new journalist to us. This is Tabby Jóhannsson. And that is Andri, Tabby's brother and Gabriella's—"

"The man who let her walk away," Lena interjected. She raised a brow and nudged the woman beside her. "You know what we do to men like that, Carrie."

"He's not Buck." Carrie pursed her lips. "Because if he is..."

"He's not," Gabriella said hastily, and Andri's heart swelled.

"*Bene.*" Gio said, appearing beside him, Tabby's trunk in his arms. Then he lowered his voice, "The man Carrie would marry left her. She has not found him."

Gio took the trunk upstairs as the women continued a dizzying conversation in the wallpapered foyer. Andri bemoaned his leg that he had to allow another man to carry Gabby's and his sister's trunks. At least Freya had returned to settle at his feet.

"Tabitha is not our only new journalist." A tiny, dark-haired woman walked beside Gio down the steps. "Come into the parlor and meet Klara and Liesl. Gio, take Andri's trunk with you and we will talk later."

"*Si, signora.*" Gio tipped his flatcap, then caught Andri's arm. "You will be much happy here."

Before Andri found words to reply, the man winked and dashed across the street, disappearing into the crowd. "I don't want to like him."

Gabby chuckled. "You and every other eligible bachelor. He flirts, but someday he'll find a girl who wins his heart."

Andri hugged her close. "Or perhaps he's found that girl, but doesn't feel worthy of her. I can hardly believe you love me, Gabby. After—"

She put a finger over his lips. "Secrets and youth do not make a good combination. Honesty and the wisdom that comes with age, however?" She kissed his cheek, then led him inside.

They convened in the parlor and Andri's head nearly spun with all the conversations going on around him. Eight women with so many differing personalities. As he watched each in turn, he felt his admiration grow. From the German girl, Liesl, with camera at her side, to Lena with her shrewd gaze. Tabby's bright-faced youth seemed to soak in every one of Ali's words. Emma peppered Klara, a homely-looking woman, with questions about her work as a secretary to Ali's husband. And of course his Gabby, who compared notes with Carrie about Detective Arthur's investigation.

He wasn't sure when it happened, exactly, but he found Ali at his side, a kind smile lighting her eyes.

"I'm glad you've come, Andri." Ali's gaze dropped to his knee. "How is it? Do you need medicine or rest for it? I'm sure travel was difficult."

"I'll survive." Andri knew she'd see through his words, but offered them anyway.

"My husband's preferred physician will call on you tomorrow. Do not worry about payment. His services are one benefit of being part of my agency."

"Part of—Me?" Andri pointed to himself. "Part of your agency?"

"Considering the way you look at our Gabriella, I

assume you have a proposal in mind." Ali eyed him.

Andri glanced over his shoulder, ensuring Gabby was distracted. He lowered his voice. "With your permission, yes. Since Gabby has no parents, I wished to formally ask you for her hand."

Ali smiled. "Good. You have it. You've proven yourself, Andri. And with that in mind, I'd like to offer you a position here."

"I had an idea about that." He glanced at his knee. "If I may?"

Ali motioned him to go ahead.

"I'd like to be a doorman of sorts and offer my protection to your journalists. I cannot chase after a thief until, or unless, my knee heals ... but my bulk intimidates without effort. And of course Freya guards well." He patted his dog's head.

"Then we are of similar mind. Once you propose, you may tell Gabby. Or I will. I'd like the two of you to become the keepers of this building and make it into a home. These young women are strong and determined, but I am aging and cannot always be on hand to guide them."

"Or protect them?"

Ali nodded. "I saw this clearly with Gabriella's situation. I never want a young woman here alone again. Crime is escalating along with the unemployment rate. My journalists need someone to keep their home secure so they can do what they've been called to do."

Peace engulfed Andri's spirit. "I believe you've read my mind, Mrs. Di Stasio."

"Ali." She winked. "You and my Griff will get along famously, I'm sure. Gio will return later to take you to his mother's home."

Andri hesitated.

"Don't worry. It's only a few blocks into the Little Italy neighborhood. Perhaps it will spur you to propose sooner, eh?" Andri felt his face flush hot and Ali grinned. She turned to the room at large and clapped her hands. "Ladies, let's get Tabby settled in her room and leave our lovebirds for a moment."

Tabby grinned at them, then called for Freya to join her and they followed the other journalists out of the room, leaving him alone with Gabby. She tucked herself into his side. Andri relaxed against the sofa back, stretching his sore leg out in front of him. "It's going to get awful hard to leave you each night, if tonight is a foreshadowing."

"And what do you have in mind to solve that problem?" Gabby tilted her face up to him. So close he could kiss her lips.

"Marry me?" He hadn't meant to ask it so bluntly, so soon, but he didn't regret the question. Not one bit.

"Are you truly alright staying here in the city?" She searched his face. "I love you, Andri. I couldn't bear it if you turn out to be miserable."

He kissed her. Quick and firm. "I could never be miserable if I'm with you. Anyway, Ali offered me a position as official security and doorman for the Di Stasio building."

Gabriella giggled, then sobered. "You're being serious."

"She wants us to make this place into a home and look after the journalists so they can do their jobs as only you ladies can do." It was his turn to study her and make sure this plan was something she wanted. He could see the idea weave through her mind, then drip down into her heart. It must have met a fertile field there because a smile blossomed.

"It's a lovely idea, Andri." She sat up, excitement animating her. "Carrie asked if I could do a sketch for her. Perhaps I can do more of those for the others, too. I don't want to illustrate galas anymore. And if we're married, I wouldn't have to. I could help the others with their investigations. Oh Andri, I love this idea."

Andri grinned and cupped her cheek. "Enough to say yes?"

"To what?" Gabby clapped hands over her mouth with a gasp, apparently just now realizing she had never answered his proposal.

Andri laughed, pried her hands from her lips, and kissed her soundly. "I'll ask again, Miss Salatino. Will you marry me?"

"Yes, yes. It was never a question, Andri. As long as we're together, that's the best dream I could ever have."

He kissed her once, twice more. "Then be sure to sketch it in the morning."

Continue the series in ...
Sabotage Games
Read on for an excerpt.

SABOTAGE GAMES

CHICAGO, ILL., JAN. 14, 1932—"Emma!"

"For the third time, I'm coming, Lena!" Emma Hancock shouted back as she stuffed her baseball glove into her satchel, then tossed the strap over her shoulder as she headed for the stairs, skirt swishing around her knees.

"We have a train to catch." Redheaded Lena Carney stood at the base of the steps, arms crossed, looking smart in her tan trench coat. "The cab's waiting with our luggage."

Emma rolled her eyes, dropping the satchel so she could shrug into her gray wool coat. Freya, the agency's German Shepherd, sniffed her bag. While Emma adored her fellow journalists, Lena needed to smile more. The political journalist was too serious. That's why Emma preferred covering sports.

"*Le mie stelline*," their boss chided. Ali Di Stasio founded the Di Stasio Giornaliste agency after she married the wealthy Griff Morland about four decades ago. She kept her maiden surname as her professional pseudonym since Griff's upper-class neighbors would not approve of his wife's undercover exploits.

"I am never early, but I am seldom late." Emma covered her dark curls with her bright red knit hat. "Anyway, there was a game at Chicago Stadium last night."

Lena stared. Freya leaned against Lena's leg, tongue lolling.

"Hockey game. Black Hawks hosted the Montreal Canadiens." Emma huffed, then realized the hall had crowded with half of the agency's six journalists and Gabby's new husband. "We lost, by the way. Two one."

"Train, Emma." Lena sighed, the long-suffering colleague. Drat her.

"Fine." Emma wrapped her matching red scarf around her neck. Her coat might be gray, but the rest of her accessories didn't need to be colorless. "Off we go then."

"*Primo, una preghierina*." Ali's Italian words brought immediate peace to Emma's soul and the room. One would never realize Ali was once an Italian street urchin, what with her cultured tone, and well-dressed manner.

Until she brought God into the conversation, then her Italian flared, both in words and accent.

It always caught Emma off guard, this apparent closeness Ali had with the Almighty. Emma didn't have time for such revenant demand. Except when Ali huddled them close.

The diminutive woman rested one hand on Emma's head, the other on Lena's as she offered a prayer of blessing over them and their mission. She sent her journalists off in such a manner only when they went undercover or on an extended trip.

This particular trip would last over a month, perhaps longer for Lena depending on what campaign trail she would need to follow. Apparently, the governor of New York State had declared a run for president. Mr. Roosevelt would also open the Olympic Games, so Lena elbowed her way into Emma's trip.

The gathered women, and Gabby's husband, all echoed Ali's amen, then Andri opened the front door, ordering Freya to stay. Gabriella Salitino, a talented sketch artist, had married her childhood friend Andri Jóhannsson over Christmas, and they were now the resident chaperones. Never a necessity before, but Emma had to admit that with the rising unemployment rate, it was nice having a former police officer and his dog living in the house now.

Lena herded them toward the waiting cab outside, watchfulness tensing the line of her shoulders as she eyed the breadline winding around St. Mark's Catholic Church across the street.

"Do you have all the information you need?" Andri followed them down the brownstone steps, Freya at his side. "Yesterday, I spoke with the owner of the home where you'll be staying. They will expect you Saturday evening."

"I called Mrs. Callahan as well," Lena said as the cab driver opened the rear car door. "I will be coming and going between there and Albany, so she is providing me a separate room. With Governor Roosevelt tossing his hat into the democratic nomination ring, I need to learn more about the man."

"Wait." Emma held up both hands as if under arrest. "Callahan?"

"Emma." Lena rolled her eyes. "We've known their name for weeks."

"No. No I haven't. I would have remembered." She had a mind for names and stats and dates, and this name, she would have remembered. "Callahan is the name of one of the female speed skaters taking part in the demonstration."

"Fortuitous, then?" Andri winked at her. "Or perhaps Ali suggested this house because she knew the connection."

Lena smirked as she slid into the cab. Emma's shoulders sank. "Ali is like a spider with her web. It probably extends to Europe!"

"I suspect it does." Andri chuckled, but gave Emma a nudge into the car. "Off with you now. The train won't wait. Remember, if you need anything, call the telephone line, send a telegraph the house, release a carrier—"

"Pigeon, I know." Emma laughed.

A cold January wind blew itself under her skirt, and she slapped her palms on it before climbing into the cab and settling her satchel at her feet. Her spirits soared nearly as high as the fabric had as the cabby sped down the Chicago streets toward Union Station.

In less than an hour, they would begin the train journey across the United States to upstate New York, to a small town on Lake Placid and the third Winter Olympiad.

Continue reading
Sabotage Games
daniellegrandinetti.com/sabotage-games

FROM THE AUTHOR

Dear Reader,

Thank you for reading Gabby and Andri's story. I hope you enjoyed reading their second-chance romance.

This story grew out of my research into Wisconsin's prohibition history. While Wisconsin originally supported the 18th Amendment, the negative economic impact quickly reversed that support. Brewing companies created workarounds like beer kits, which came with a "warning" that said if left to ferment, it could create alcohol. Eventually, state law enforcement stopped enforcing the amendment, leaving it up to federal or local officers to handle, and lawmakers began working to repeal it from the Constitution.

There was one town, however, that stood stalwart

against alcohol within city limits so that in 1994, it became the last dry town in the state of Wisconsin. Then, in 2016, after over one-hundred-sixty years, Ephriam voted to allow the sale of alcohol in town. Now, that got my creative "what-if" juices flowing! Ephriam is located in Door County, the peninsula that juts out into Lake Michigan, and I thought, what if I created a fictional town with a similar history?

Door County has fascinated me since I was little. Growing up in the Chicagoland area, it seemed half of those who had summer cottages went to Door County. The tip of Door County is a dangerous shipping passage for boats bound for Green Bay, so dangerous it got the name Porte des Morts, or Death's Door. The "door" part being why the county has its name. In the late 1800s, a straight was dug at the base of the peninsula, in Sturgeon Bay, which allows ships to bypass Porte des Morts. However, what if I set my dry town on a fictional island in that now-infrequently traveled passage?

With a tangible plan for setting a fictional town on the peninsula, I dug into the history of the actual islands surrounding Death's Door. Like understanding Washington Island and Plum Island, where the lighthouses stand, and which people groups have lived there. They were originally populated by the Potawatomi and the Ojibwa tribes, then added Scandinavians, especially Icelandic immigrants. With that in mind, Andri's name is of Icelandic descent.

Gabby is a journalist with the fictional Di Stasio Giornaliste Agency, founded by Ali Di Stasio. If you missed the story of the agency's founder, you can find it in the prequel novella *Undercover Wish*. Then stay tuned for Emma's Olympic-sized adventure when the sports reporter travels to Lake Placid, NY, and then L.A. for the 1932 Winter and Summer Olympic Games in *Sabotage Games*.

Special thanks to Sarah Hinkle and Bethany Aich for making this story shine. And a great big thank you to my husband and boys for giving me the time to turn these thoughts into a story for you. If you've enjoyed *Eyewitness Sketch*, I'd be most grateful if you'd take a moment to leave an honest review.

What more from Ali? I'm growing a paid dispatch on Substack with her notes, vignettes, and flash fiction stories. Visit daniellegrandinetti.com/wire to learn more.

Thank you again for joining me for Gabby and Andri's investigation!

Happy reading!
Danielle Grandinetti

JOIN MY FIRESIDE NEWS

Grab a spot on my virtual hearth and receive a weekly email filled with bookish content. As a thank you for subscribing, you'll receive a digital copy of my historical romance novelette: *Fire and Water*.

Subscribe Here

Di Stasio Giornaliste Agency

La Verità con Integrità. Truth with Integrity.
The Legacy of a (Girl) Stunt Reporter.
daniellegrandinetti.com/di-stasio-giornaliste-agency

Undercover Wish

Di Stasio Giornaliste Agency, #0
Alessandra Di Stasio
Chicago World's Fair: World's Columbian Exposition

Eyewitness Sketch

Di Stasio Giornaliste Agency, #1

DANIELLE GRANDINETTI

Gabriella Salatino
Prohibition

Sabotage Games

DI STASIO GIORNALISTE AGENCY, #2
Emma Hancock
Summer & Winter Olympics: Lake Placid & L.A.

Shrouded Trail

DI STASIO GIORNALISTE AGENCY, #3
Lena Carney
Presidential Election

Fraudulent Progress

DI STASIO GIORNALISTE AGENCY, #4
Klara James
Chicago World's Fair: A Century Of Progress Exposition

Pursuing Dust

DI STASIO GIORNALISTE AGENCY, #5
Tabitha Jóhannsson
Dust Bowl

EYEWITNESS SKETCH

Hostile Ally

Di Stasio Giornaliste Agency, #6
Liesl Kaufman
Berlin Olympics

HARBORED IN CROW'S NEST

Welcome to Crow's Nest,
where danger and romance meet at the water's edge.
daniellegrandinetti.com/harbored-in-crows-nest

Confessions to a Stranger

HARBORED IN CROW'S NEST, #1
*She's lost her future. He's sacrificed his.
Now they have a chance to reclaim it—together.*

Refuge for the Archaeologist

HARBORED IN CROW'S NEST, #2

DANIELLE GRANDINETTI

*Will uncovering the truth set them free
or destroy what they hold most dear?*

Escape with the Prodigal

HARBORED IN CROW'S NEST, #3
*Only a Christmas miracle will save
an unwed mother and the lumberjack protecting her.*

Relying on the Enemy

HARBORED IN CROW'S NEST, #4
*She's protecting her children.
He's redeeming his past.*

Sheltered by the Doctor

HARBORED IN CROW'S NEST, #5
*A fake relationship might keep her safe,
but will it break their hearts?*

Investigation of a Journalist

HARBORED IN CROW'S NEST, #6
*A second chance to set the record straight,
and rekindle a lost love.*

Unexpected Protectors

Visit small-town Wisconsin during the Dairy Strikes of the Great Depression in these three historical romances.

For details, visit:
daniellegrandinetti.com/unexpected-protectors

To Stand in the Breach

STRIKE TO THE HEART, #1
She came to America to escape a workhouse prison, but will the cost of freedom be too high a price to pay?

DANIELLE GRANDINETTI

A Strike to the Heart

STRIKE TO THE HEART, #2

She's fiercely independent.
He's determined to protect her.

As Silent as the Night

STRIKE TO THE HEART, #3

He can procure anything, except his heart's deepest wish.
She might hold the key, if she's not discovered first.

FAIRYTALE RETELLINGS

HEART OF BEAUTY
stand-alone origin novella

Discover the origin of Crooked Tooth Ranch in this 1870s western retelling of Beauty and the Beast.

daniellegrandinetti.com/heart-of-beauty

HIS BOSS'S LITTLE SISTER
stand-alone novella in the Apron Strings Tea

DANIELLE GRANDINETTI

Tale multi-author series

A touch of fairy tale, a spoonful of history, and a teacup of hope ... a 1930s historical romance retelling of Hansel and Gretel.

daniellegrandinetti.com/his-bosss-little-sister

UNDERCOVER WISH
stand-alone novella, part of the Di Stasio Giornaliste Agency series

A Di Stasio Giornaliste Agency origin story and a retelling of Aladdin and the Magic Lamp.

daniellegrandinetti.com/heart-of-beauty

Our House Novellas

As the world marches toward what will become WWII, visit Our House as we join the resistance.

The Italian Musician's Sanctuary
Romance, history and intrigue at Our House on Sycamore Street.

Hunted by one man, can she open her heart to another?
Eden Cove, England, 1931—Margherita Vicienzo flees Italy pursued by her former fiancé, a member of Mussolini's Blackshirt. Smuggled illegally into England, Margherita is a foreigner at the mercy of strangers. Her limp from an improperly healed broken leg means she has nothing to offer the Ferryman family, who offer her

sanctuary, and nothing to appease their son who resents her presence.

Luke Ferryman needs a wife. He wants to marry for love, but carries the weight of his family's generations-old expectations on his shoulders. Though he inherited the role of both baker and ferryman, he knows he can't fulfill both needs once his aging grandparents retire. A wife would help, but not an illegal one like the refugee his matchmaking grandmother is harboring.

As opposite as night and day, Luke and Margherita forge a tentative friendship that grows despite the constant threat of Margherita's discovery. But when strangers appear in the close-knit seaside town, threatening Luke's livelihood and Margherita's safety, the choice between justice and mercy becomes harder. And sacrifice proves the only answer.

The Recluse's Vindication
Rumors, Monsters, and Second Chances at
Our House on Heather Wynd

The Loch Ness Monster isn't the only recluse seeking a Scottish haven.

Bieldfell, Scotland, 1933—Falsely accused of murder sixteen years ago, American cowboy Benjamin Ford has chosen to hide out in the Scottish Highlands. Reclusive and not afraid to die, he rescues children out of an increasingly dangerous Germany. When his childhood best friend appears at his door, he's not the boy she remembers.

Eleanor Finch's life ended sixteen years ago. In one horrible day, she lost her dreams, her reputation, and her heart. However, she never gives up the hope of finding her friend, so when she learns of Ben's whereabouts, she leaves all that is familiar to convince him to return home.

But Eleanor isn't the only person searching for Ben. Hunters follow her trail. The thin veil of gossip and rumor may be their only chance of a future ... unless the Loch Ness Monster is real after all.

daniellegrandinetti.com/our-house

ABOUT THE AUTHOR

Danielle Grandinetti is an award-winning author of 1930s historical romance, where mystery and suspense intertwine with hope. Her work has received recognition including a Distinguished Faith in Writing Award, two National Excellence in Storytelling Awards, and finalist honors in the FHLCW Reader's Choice, Selah, and Daphne du Maurier contests.

DANIELLE GRANDINETTI

A second-generation Italian-American rooted in Midwest traditions, Danielle draws inspiration from tea, books, and the creative beauty of nature. Holding a master's in communication and culture, and driven by a lifelong love of stories, she crafts tales that celebrate resilience, diversity, and belonging. Danielle lives along Wisconsin's Lake Michigan shoreline with her husband and two sons. Find her online at daniellegrandinetti.com.

RIGHT YOUR WRONGS

KINGS OF THE ICE 6

KANDI STEINER

Copyright (C) 2025 Kandi Steiner
All rights reserved.

No part of this book may be used or reproduced in any form or by any means, electronic or mechanical, including photocopying, recording, or by any information storage and retrieval system without prior written consent of the author except where permitted by law.

The characters and events depicted in this book are fictitious. Any similarity to real persons, living or dead, is coincidental and not intended by the author.

Published by Kandi Steiner, LLC
Edited by Elaine York/Allusion Publishing, www.allusionpublishing.com
Cover Photography by Ren Saliba
Cover Design by Kandi Steiner
Formatting by Elaine York/Allusion Publishing, www.allusionpublishing.com